MARRIED UNDER THE MISTLETOE

HOLLIE LUCKIE

Book Cover by Dirty Girl Designs

Proofread by Caroline Palmier | Love and Edits

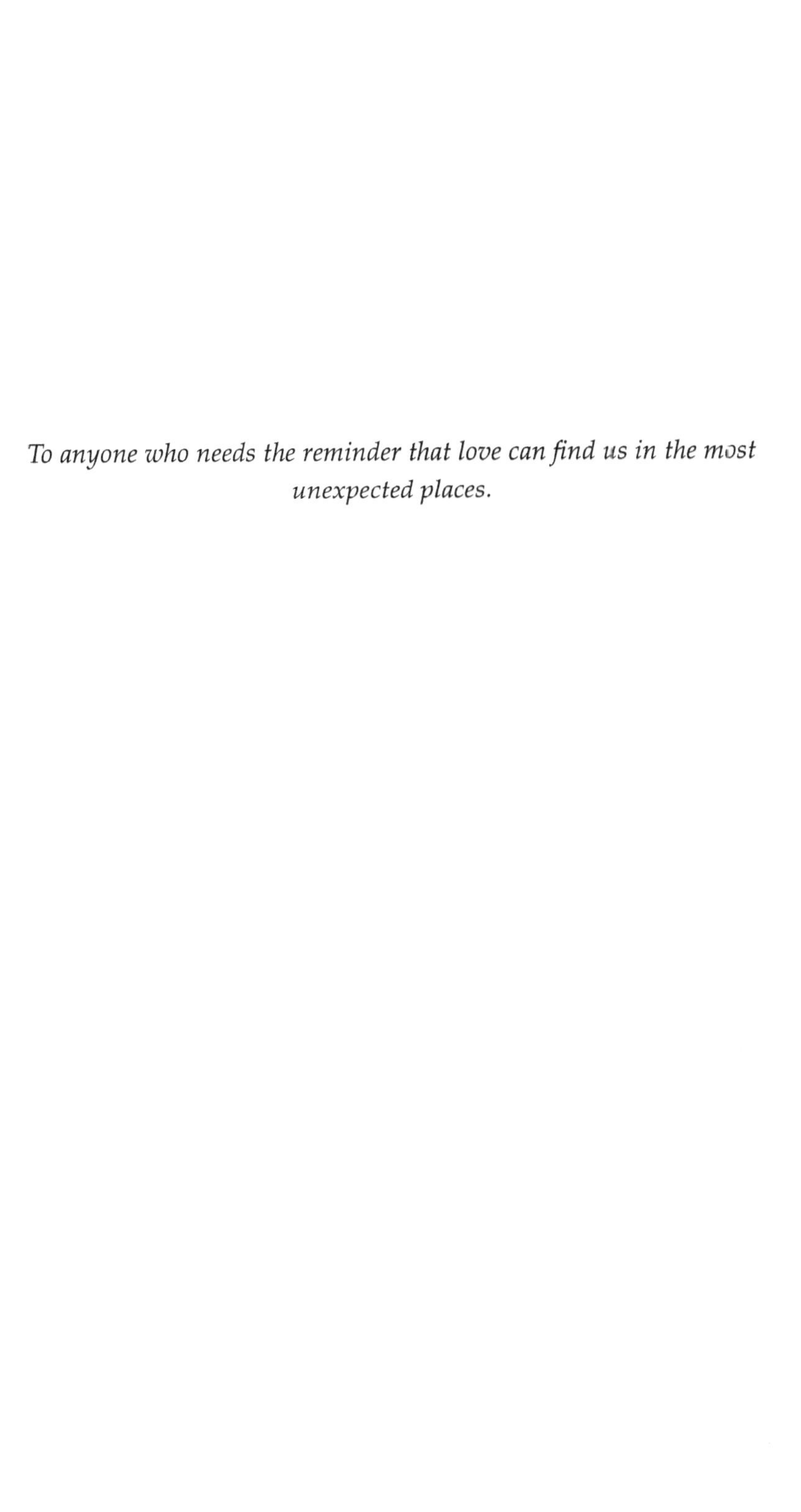

To anyone who needs the reminder that love can find us in the most unexpected places.

PLAYLIST

Frost on the Pines by Joe Jordan
A Nonsense Christmas by Sabrina Carpenter
Can't Help Falling in Love by Kacey Musgraves
Santa Tell Me by Ariana Grande
Everywhere, Everything by Noah Kahan and Gracie Abrams
Ribbons and Bows by Kacey Musgraves
All My Love by Noah Kahan
Blue Christmas by Megan Moroney
I Don't Wanna Live Forever by ZAYN and Taylor Swift
Snow's Not The Only Thing Falling by Patrick Murphy
You Are My Sunshine by Jasmine Thompson
If I Ain't Got You by Alicia Keys
Present Without A Bow by Kacey Musgraves and Leon Bridges

AUTHOR'S NOTE

Thank you so much for reading *Married Under the Mistletoe*. Bridget and Easton's story is so much fun, and I'm so excited to share it with you. This book is full of small town chaos, spice, and all the banter you could want. However, there are few more serious things discussed within the contents of this book.

Married Under the Mistletoe contains mature content that may not be suitable for all audiences. For a full list of content warnings, flip to the content list at the back of the book.

CHAPTER 1
BRIDGET

"You're all set! I hope you enjoyed your stay at Deer Valley Inn."

The couple across the counter smiles at each other, and I try not to cringe at the knowing looks they're sharing

"Oh my gosh, it was wonderful. This place is so romantic. I can see why so many people want to get married here. This visit was the best early Christmas present I could've asked for, honey," the woman says, pulling her husband down for a quick kiss.

"Yeah, we haven't felt this connected in years," the man agrees, looking down at his wife with a smile.

I continue to fight the urge to cringe at the looks they're sending each other just before they lean in for another kiss.

It's fine, just another day here at Deer Valley.

The couple finally pulls themselves apart, and the wife reaches down to grab the invoice off the counter.

"Sorry, honey. He's just so handsome, I have a hard time keeping my hands to myself. I'm sure you know how that is."

Actually, I don't.

At twenty-nine, I've never felt more painfully single in my life than I have over the last two years. Deer Valley has really taken off with the help of my cousin's new wife, Millie. But it turns out that working at an inn famous for its weddings comes with its downfalls. It seems like everyone is in love, while I'm left eating chocolate alone in my bed at the end of every day.

I force a smile and laugh. "No worries. I'm glad you all had such a good time. We'd love to have you back anytime."

"Oh, we'll definitely be back. It's too bad y'all stay so booked up, though. But I guess that's great for y'all, isn't it?"

"We definitely don't complain," I tell her honestly. "The holidays are our busiest season."

The woman looks around at the Christmas decorations filling the lobby and laughs. "Yes, well I can definitely see why. I've never seen a town that gets this into decorating. But it's absolutely beautiful, and oh my gosh, that gingerbread latte from the coffee shop tasted like Christmas in a cup."

"Yes, that's one of my favorites," I agree.

"Well, thank you again, and we'll see you soon," the woman says. Her husband smiles and nods in acknowledgement before wrapping his arm around his wife and leading her out of the lobby.

As soon as they're gone, I blow out a breath and rub my eyes in exhaustion. The last few weeks have been incredibly busy, and with the huge wedding we have coming in this weekend, there doesn't seem to be any rest in sight.

Standing from my seat at the counter, I smile at the guests milling around in the lobby as I make my way over to the restaurant. Isabelle, the hostess, smiles at me as soon she sees me, gesturing me over.

"Hey, Bridget. How are you? Do you ever leave this place?

I'm pretty sure you've been here every day for the last two weeks."

I laugh, trying not to think about the fact that she's right. I've been working more than ever over the last few weeks, trying to keep things afloat while my cousin Brian and his new wife Millie are on their honeymoon.

"Well, since Brian decided to get married during our busiest season of the year, I haven't had much of a choice," I say.

"I guess that's true. Their wedding last weekend looked like something out of a movie. I've never seen the inn so beautiful," Isabelle gushes. "I just can't believe after two years they're finally married. When are they getting back in town?"

"Millie texted me this morning that they were on their way to the airport. So they should be back in plenty of time for the big Barnes wedding this weekend," I answer.

"I can't believe how big of an event that wedding has turned into. And all the reporters that are coming into town? It's gonna be wild!" Isabelle says with wide eyes.

I nod in agreement. "Yeah, Millie told me we're expected to be the cover story for *Weddings and Wine*. Can you believe it? I mean, they featured us in an article two years ago and that's what started the whole wedding craze here. But the cover? That's wild. We're gonna be so crazy booked we won't know what to do with ourselves."

Isabelle laughs, nodding in agreement. "Yeah, it's gonna be so much fun. Aren't there other reporters coming too?"

"Yes, there are also reporters from *Southern Weddings* and *Bama Brides*. I just can't believe Millie managed to pull it all together. I know it's something she's been working on forever."

"Well, you know how she is. Once she sets her mind to

something, I'd hate to be the one to stand in her way. I mean who else do you know that could pull off a wedding full of fake snow in the middle of South Alabama. She had this place looking like a winter wonderland."

"Yeah, it was really beautiful," I agree. "But I think the first weekend in December was cutting it a little close for our holiday crowd."

Isabelle nods. "I can agree with that. Every year, I think there's no way this place could get any busier around the holidays, and each year, I'm proven wrong. I'm pretty sure there's been over two hundred guests through the restaurant today, and it's only lunch time."

I laugh. "You know, ever since Miss Sally put the word out about the eggnog French toast, we can't seem to keep the locals out of this place."

Isabelle chuckles, and I step aside to let her greet the party that just arrived for an early lunch. While I wait for her to return, I pull out my phone and check my texts from Millie.

Millie: Hey, so I have bad news.

Millie: It's not the worst news in the world, but you're definitely not going to be very happy.

Millie: But just remember you love me

Millie: And you're so happy for Brian and I…

I blow out a breath, preparing myself for what she's going to say next.

Bridget: Hit me with it…

Millie: We're snowed in.

Millie: I know I probably should have seen
this coming, but you know I've always
wanted to visit New York at Christmas. And
Brian and I have had the best time on our
honeymoon. This place is truly magical.

Millie: But some major storm just came
through, and it's looking like we're gonna be
stuck here for a couple more days.

I freeze, putting together a mental timeline in my head.

Bridget: Millie…

Bridget: The Barnes wedding is in just
THREE DAYS.

Bridget: You know, the biggest wedding of
the season?!

Millie: I know, I know.

Millie: But it's going to be just fine. We're set
to fly in Friday morning, and I'll be there to
help you put the finishing touches on
everything. But I just need you to help make
sure everything goes smoothly in the
meantime.

I take a deep breath and try to remind myself this isn't the
end of the world. But with all the added pressure of the
reporters, the Barnes wedding this weekend has the potential
to really make or break our next season, and we need it to go
perfectly.

Millie: Bridget, you know I wouldn't ask you
to do this if I didn't believe in you. I promise
you're ready to do this. So can I count on
you to take over…at least until I get back?

Looking down at my phone, I realize my hands are trembling, and I force myself to take a few calming breaths. Before Millie rolled into town two years ago, I'd helped handle most of the events and I've really enjoyed learning from her. I know I can do this, but the added pressure and the fear of letting everyone down does feel a little crippling. After pulling myself together, I type out a response to Millie.

> Bridget: Don't worry about a thing. I promise we're gonna knock the Christmas socks off those reporters.

Millie: That's the spirit!

Millie: You know where the binder of all the details is in my office. Look over it, and I'll call you tomorrow with more information.

Millie: Thank you Bridget. You're the best! Since we're stranded here, Brian surprised me with tickets to a last minute show on Broadway.

> Bridget: I can tell you're really suffering by not being able to come home, huh?

> Bridget: I'm kidding. Go enjoy the show. And tell my cousin that he owes me big time.

Millie: Already on it. Love you!

> Bridget: Love you!

Tucking my phone in my pocket, I sigh as I make my way back over to the check in desk, stopping in Millie's office to grab the huge binder of plans for the Barnes wedding. Resigning myself to the fact that I won't be getting much sleep tonight, I start to read through her notes. It looks like I've got a wedding to coordinate.

CHAPTER 2
EASTON

"All right, I think we're good for the night. I'll wrap up everything here," I say, turning to Chance, my best friend and the bartender at Deer Valley.

"You sure? I don't mind sticking around if you need help," Chance answers, looking around at the mess I've managed to make in the kitchen.

"Yeah, man. I'm sure, but I appreciate it. I'm gonna do one last test run on the crab cake appetizers for the wedding this weekend before I leave, but I'll see you tomorrow."

Chance nods as he slips on his brown Carhartt jacket and grimaces as he looks out at the cold December night through the window of the kitchen. "You know, I really don't love the cold weather we're getting this year."

I laugh as I load one of the dishwashers. "Yeah, me either. There's a reason I moved from Wisconsin, and the main one was the whole warm weather thing."

"Well, you know if you wait about two weeks it'll be hot as hell again," Chance teases.

"Yeah, I don't think I'll ever get used to these Alabama

winters. Didn't it snow around this time a couple years ago?" I ask.

"Yep, that's how Brian met Millie. We also got a little bit at Christmas last year, and I wouldn't be surprised if we get some this year. Just get ready for your first Christmas in Springside, man. I've lived here for my whole life, and I still can't believe how into everything this town gets."

"Well, I kind of started to put that together last month when the town put on its own version of the Macy's Thanksgiving Day Parade. I've never seen so many balloons in my life," I muse, starting the dishwasher and turning back to my best friend.

Chance shrugs. "Well, what can we say? We're a festive bunch around here."

"I'm seeing that. So help me get prepared. What can I expect from the Christmas festivities this year?" I ask curiously. "I feel like we've been so focused on the weddings over the last few weeks, but it's already the second week in December. "

"Oh, let's see. I don't know if you've heard about it with the way you stay holed up in this kitchen, but Millie is planning Seven Days of Springside Christmas."

I blink at him in confusion. "Seven? What happened to twelve?"

"I asked the same thing, but she said she's working her way up. Her first year there were two, and last year there were four," Chance explains.

"Um, wouldn't six have been the more logical choice, then?" I ask with a laugh.

"You know Millie," Chance says simply, and I nod.

From what I've been told, Brian's new wife took over the events at Deer Valley after getting stuck in town due to a freak snow storm two years ago, and she's been a big part of turning the inn into one of the most popular couples destinations in the south. She and Brian have both been incredible since I moved here, and I know if she's in charge of the events, they'll be perfectly planned.

"Okay, so what's included in these seven days?" I ask.

Chance pauses thoughtfully before starting to count off the events on his fingers. "Let's see. There's always the Mistletoe Maze and the Gingerbread Gala. And then last year she added the Candy Cane Carnival and the Cookie Celebration."

"Um, why do I suddenly feel like I'm in the middle of a Hallmark movie?" I laugh, shaking my head.

Chance shrugs as he continues. "And then this year she's adding Sledding with Santa, an ugly sweater competition, and some kind of movie night."

"Wow, that's quite the list," I say as he finishes. "But first we have to get through the Barnes wedding this weekend. I've been making hors d'oeuvres for days."

"Yeah, I guess they'll all start piling in over the next few days. Every time I think we can't get any busier, I look up and there's a line out the door to be seated."

I nod. "Yeah, I've got to talk to Brian and Bridget about getting more help around here. The small team of guys I have back here are great, but if we're gonna keep going at this pace, I need at least five or six more. I know we're a small restaurant, but between the events and the restaurant, I'm doing more than double the work I did at the bigger restaurants in the city."

Chance nods in agreement. "Yeah, I wouldn't say no to another bartender or two either. I bet Brian and Bridget would be up for it if we can find someone."

"What would we be up for?" Bridget asks, making her way into the kitchen.

"Oh, hey, Bridget," I say. "We were just saying if we're gonna stay as busy as we've been over the last few months, we'd like to talk to you about getting some extra staff for both of us."

"Yeah, I think we can definitely do that," Bridget agrees, collapsing in the small chair over in the corner.

Chance's phone rings in his pocket, and he looks down at it, shaking his head. "It's my mom. I've gotta go. See y'all tomorrow."

He turns, answering his phone as he goes, leaving Bridget and I alone in the kitchen. Bridget comes in to chat with me at the end of the day most nights, and I'd be lying if I said I didn't look forward to it. I'm pretty sure it started as her checking in on me, but over the last few months, I'd like to believe we've become good friends.

"Ugh, I'm exhausted." Bridget sighs, rubbing her eyes.

I look at her, noticing the dark circles under her eyes and the chaotic way her usually perfectly styled hair is piled on the top of her head.

"I bet you are. I've been getting in early to start prepping everything for the wedding on Saturday, and I've seen your car here every morning when I come in. You've also been here every night when I shut down the kitchen. Are you even leaving? Eating? Sleeping?" I ask, trying to mask the concern in my voice.

I know it's not my place to worry about her, but the truth is I've developed a small crush on Bridget over the last few months. I'd never act on it because she's technically my boss, but she makes me laugh and she's so easy to talk to. Plus, not to mention, with her long brown hair and green eyes, she's the most beautiful girl I've ever laid eyes on.

"Um, not really," she admits tiredly. "I've been going home and grabbing a few hours of sleep here and there, but I don't think I've eaten anything since breakfast unless you count the sugar cookie and the gingerbread latte I grabbed from the coffee corner around two."

"I don't," I say, shaking my head at her. "Okay, this is what we're gonna do. You're gonna sit here and let me whip you up something to eat. And then when you're done, you're gonna go home and sleep for at least eight hours. I mean it. I don't want to hear a word about you coming in before ten tomorrow."

Bridget's eyes widen in surprise. "You don't have to do that. I know you're ready to get out of here. Plus, I need to make sure the seating chart's approved and send another email to the band to make sure they got the list of songs the bride requested they play on Saturday."

"I don't mind. And that can wait," I insist, walking over to the refrigerator. "Isn't Marie working reception in the morning? Pretty sure I remember seeing that on the schedule."

"Yeah, she is," Bridget says.

I lean into the large stainless fridge to grab what I need to make her something to eat. Deciding to throw together a cranberry and brie grilled cheese, I grab the mozzarella, brie, and cranberry sauce before turning back to the counter.

"See. Let her take the early morning check ins, sleep in just a little bit, and hit it hard tomorrow after you've had some rest. And a sandwich," I tease.

"I'll think about it," Bridget sighs. "I knew it would be a challenge taking care of everything without Brian and Millie, but I don't think I was prepared for just how hard it would be. And now they're snowed in, and we have this major wedding on Saturday. I know we've cut things close around here before, but I don't know how I'm gonna do it all by myself."

"You don't have to do it alone. There's an entire staff of

people in this hotel who can help you," I remind her as I turn on the eye of the stove.

She nods. "I guess you're right."

I throw some butter in the pan and sit the sandwich on top before turning back to her.

"I'm here for whatever you need, Bridget." I tell her truthfully.

She smiles at me, and I try not to think about the fact that she's sitting less than a few feet away from me in the shadows of the kitchen. "Thanks, Easton," she says. "By the way, one of these days I'm gonna need to slip in here to try this eggnog french toast you keep making. Miss Sally has the whole town buzzing about it."

I laugh as I flip the sandwich, and Bridget groans behind me. "God, that smells so good."

"God, I've never been so sick of smelling syrup in my life," I tease. "But come by anytime, and I'll fix it for you."

We sit in comfortable silence while I finish her food, and she smiles up at me as I slide it in front of her.

"Thanks again for this,"she says, grabbing the sandwich and taking a bite. "Oh my god, this is a million times better than the cereal I was planning to eat when I got home."

"Glad to hear it," I tell her truthfully. "Now, finish that and go get some sleep, please."

CHAPTER 3
BRIDGET

"You know, Bridget. You're the most beautiful woman I've ever seen," Easton whispers, turning from his spot at the stove and holding out his hand to help me up.

I stand from my chair in the corner, and he wraps his arms around me, pulling me close. "I haven't wanted to tell you this because I never want you to feel pressured, but I really like spending time with you," he whispers, brushing a piece of hair back from my face. "But there's something I've been dying to do."

He leans in and our lips graze. My heart races as his lips touch mine, and I reach out to pull him closer.

He kisses me hard, and I resist the urge to moan at how good his mouth feels against mine. After a moment, he deepens the kiss and our tongues tangle. I pull him closer, and he kisses down my neck. I sigh, loving the feeling of his beard rubbing against my sensitive skin.

"I like spending time with you too," I whisper, threading my fingers through his dark hair as he moves down my body.

He pushes me against the counter, and I wrap my legs around him as he sits me on his work station.

"Pretty sure this isn't sanitary," I tease, and I feel him smile against my skin just before he pulls my sweater over my head, exposing my lacy bra with a small bow in the center.

"Damn, baby. You look perfect all wrapped up for me," he groans, pulling down the cup of my bra and sucking my nipple into his mouth.

I moan at the contact, rubbing my hips against him. "Please, Easton," I whisper, not really sure what I'm asking for, but knowing I'm desperate to feel him everywhere.

"Don't worry, sweetheart. I'm gonna make you come for me," he says, letting his hands wander between my legs.

He grazes my clit through my leggings, and I moan as his fingers tease me. Shifting my weight, he pulls me into his arms and yanks down the waistband of my leggings before sitting me back on the stainless steel counter. I let out a yelp as the cold metal touches my ass.

"If the health department visits right now, we're fucked," I whisper, and Easton laughs.

I giggle, but it dies in my throat as he slips his finger under the lace of my panties.

"Bridget, baby, you're fucking soaked for me," he groans, sliding his finger inside me.

Beep, beep, beep.

My alarm clock blares, pulling me from the dream, and I groan.

God, what the hell was that?

I rub my eyes, trying to figure out what he hell I was thinking. Sure, I've had a minor crush on Easton since he moved to town earlier this year, but I've never thought about seriously pursuing anything with him. He's the best chef we could ask for at the inn, and I would hate myself if I did anything to make him uncomfortable.

But I've never had a dream that felt that real before. I can still feel his fingers tracing circles down my spine before he stripped me bare.

My body feels hot with need, and I stand, throwing off the covers as I try to calm myself down. I've never felt like this in my life. The very limited experience I have with anything physical never left me wanting more, but this? This is a feeling I could become addicted to.

Shaking my head, I make my way into the kitchen, pausing to lean down and pet my golden retrievers, Bessie and Jennie. "Hey, sweet girls. I know, I've missed you over the last few days," I coo, as their tails thump noisily against the hardwood floor.

Their rough tongues lick my hand, and I smile down at them. Other than running in during the day to let them out and some quick pats as I run out the door, I haven't spent as much time with them as I'd like.

"Want to come to work with me today?" I ask, and both dogs immediately shoot up from their spots and start turning in excited circles at my feet.

Coming to Deer Valley is one of my dogs favorite things to do, and judging by their reactions, they're up for a little field trip today.

"Okay, okay. Let me get dressed and y'all can come with me. But the place is packed and you have to promise to be on your best behavior," I say seriously.

In response, Jennie jumps up on her hind legs and licks my face sloppily, causing me to giggle. "Now, you have to promise me you won't do that," I tell her, gently moving her so that her paws are back on the floor.

Leaving the dogs in the kitchen, I grab a protein shake

from the fridge and head back into my room to get dressed. Checking the clock, I'm shocked to see that I managed to sleep until after eight this morning. I can't remember the last time I was still at home this late in the morning, but I force myself to relax and remind myself that the inn will be fine without me for a few hours.

I turn on my favorite Christmas playlist, smiling as Kacey Musgraves starts to blast through the room as I start to do my makeup. I'm humming along to the music and finishing my mascara when my phone rings.

"Hello?" I answer without checking the caller ID.

"Hey, okay. Before I start, you have to promise not to hate me," Millie says as soon as the call connects. Her voice sounds frantic, and I immediately pause, worried something is wrong.

"Wait, Millie. Why would I hate you? What's going on?" I ask, trying not to panic.

"Well…" Millie hesitates. "The Barnes family called me this morning, and they're all stranded in Atlanta."

I blink, waiting for her to tell me she's joking. "Um, very funny, Mills," I say, forcing a laugh.

"I'm serious, Bridget," Millie sighs, and I shake my head.

"There's no way. Atlanta's only a few hours from here. How can they be stranded?" I ask, my mind racing with what she's saying.

"Bridge, have you not turned on the TV this morning?" she asks.

"Uh, no, I haven't. I just woke up. I was exhausted so I'm moving a little slower than planned," I admit, scrambling to open the news app on my phone.

Major Snowstorm Sweeps the Southeast

The Southeast is Shut Down

Major Travel Delays Expected Just in Time For the Holidays

Atlanta Airport Shut Down Due to Snowy Weather

I read through a few more of the headlines and shake my head in disbelief.

"Millie, what does this mean? What are we going to do?" I cry, rapidly starting to panic.

"Well, that's why I'm calling you," Millie says hesitantly.

"If they're not coming, what about the reporters? The features? All the flowers and food that have been ordered? Everything's just off?"

"Not exactly," Millie admits, and I blink in confusion.

"If there's no bride, no groom, and no guests, how the hell are we going to pull this off?" I ask.

"Well, I called Catherine from *Weddings and Wine* this morning. She's coming in from a wedding in Florida, so she can still make it to you. And I pitched the idea of her reporting on a small town wedding between a local newly engaged couple. She absolutely loved it.'

"Okay," I say slowly, trying to figure out where she's going with this. "But who are you talking about? I don't know of any newly engaged couples here in town. Especially none that would be willing to give up their previous wedding plans to get married in three days."

"Well, that's why I'm calling… I need you to agree to get married on Saturday," Millie admits.

I blink at the phone, waiting for her to tell me she's joking. "You're hilarious, Millie," I say, forcing a laugh. "Get married on Saturday. You almost had me."

"I'm not joking, Bridget. I would do it if I was there, but

our flight is through Atlanta so we won't be back in time. Plus the reporter knows I just got married. We talked about it when we were planning for the article."

"Millie, who the hell am I supposed to marry?" I yell, quickly panicking at the realization that she's serious.

"Calm down," Millie says calmly. "I've thought about it, and it really doesn't matter. Just think about it for a minute. It's not a real wedding. We just need you to put on a show for the reporters. Like you said, everything's already planned. Just convince one of the employees at the inn to throw on a tux and take some pictures with you. On Sunday, the reporters will leave and this will just be a really good story."

I think about what she's saying, and I slowly come to the realization that she's right. This isn't ideal, but given the current circumstances, it seems to be the best solution.

"Wait, what about a dress?" I ask, going through my head for any argument that I can think of. "There's no way I can find a dress in Springside in two days."

"You can wear mine," Millie says quickly. "We're the same size, and it's sitting across the guest bedroom at our house. My shoes and accessories are there for you too."

I hesitate, trying to come up with any other possible way to get out of this. "Millie, you know I hate being the center of attention. And this is like the epitome of the center of attention."

"I know, Bridge, but I wouldn't ask you to do this if I wasn't desperate. We're stuck here, but you know how big this feature could be for us. So, what do you say?" Millie asks, and I don't miss the desperation in her voice.

"I guess I need to find a husband then." I sigh.

CHAPTER 4
EASTON

"Hey, do you know what this is all about?" Chance asks, looking around at the lobby where half the staff of Deer Valley is gathered.

"I have no idea. I got the same text you got. I know Bridget wouldn't have called us together if it wasn't important, but I hope it doesn't last long. I left Greta in charge, but we're absolutely swamped this morning."

Chance opens his mouth to respond just as Bridget comes running into the door looking frantic. Her golden retrievers lead the way into the lobby, immediately running at Chance for attention.

"Hey, sweet girls," he murmurs, bending down to pet Bridget's dogs. "What's going on this morning, huh?"

As soon as the words are out of his mouth, Bridget clears her throat and we all turn our attention back to her. "Hey, y'all. So sorry to have to call you away from your duties this morning, but thank y'all so much for meeting me. I promise this will be quick."

She fidgets nervously, shifting from foot to foot as she

looks out at us. "So, I don't really know how to say this, but the Barnes wedding is cancelled."

The entire staff starts to whisper, looking between each other with wide eyes as we try to figure out what this means.

"But, if you didn't know, that wedding was scheduled to be our biggest wedding of the season. There are a number of reporters coming in to report on the inn, and we're counting on it to be the wedding that pushes us to the next level," Bridget says. "Millie convinced the reporters to still come, but right now, there's no wedding for them to report on."

Bridget takes a deep breath and pushes her long brown hair out of her face before blurting, "I'm asking one of you to marry me on Saturday. Or, well, pretend to marry me I guess I should say. None of it'll be real, but we need to put on a good show."

Everyone goes silent, and Chance looks at me in disbelief. "Do you think she's serious?" my best friend whispers, as Bridget continues to step nervously from foot to foot, waiting for someone to say something.

In the silence, Bridget's dogs run through the legs of Bruce, one of the custodians, almost knocking him over. The moment is just enough to break the tension in the room, and we all laugh quietly before turning our attention back to Bridget.

I can tell she's completely panicked over having to ask for help, and before I can think better of it I raise my hand. "I'll do it. Let's get hitched, Bridget."

Chance bumps my arm in shock as all the eyes in the room turn to look at me. But I keep my gaze focused on Bridget, and her face brightens.

"Are you sure?" she asks quietly, and her hesitation is the confirmation that I'm doing the right thing. If it were anyone else in the world asking for this, I would be the last to volunteer, but I'm not turning down the opportunity to spend more time with her.

"Yeah, I'm sure. It sounds like it could be fun," I lie, trying not to think about the fact that I'm signing myself up to be in the middle of whatever chaos that's about to descend upon Deer Valley.

"All right, everyone, y'all can get back to work. Thank you for letting me interrupt your day." Bridget calls out to the crowd.

People start to dissipate, and Bridget locks eyes with me. "Easton, if you're sure about this, I need to talk through a few details with you."

I nod, and Chance shakes his head at me. "Man, I knew you liked her, but I guess you really like her, huh? I'm pretty sure you're the last person I would have picked to volunteer for something like this."

I just shrug, knowing there's nothing I can say to argue with him. "Yeah, I guess. I just wanted to help her out. We both know how much stress she's been under since Brian and Millie have been gone. And I'm pretty sure all I'll have to do is wear a tux and pose for a million pictures."

"I guess," Chance says hesitantly. "I've gotta get back, but, uh, we're not done talking about this."

"Sounds great," I mumble sarcastically before turning back to Bridget who's bending over corralling her dogs back into her office.

"Oh my god, Easton, I cannot thank you enough," she blurts. "I almost came to ask you directly, but I got scared."

I smile at the admission. "No problem. I'm pretty sure I've got a tux stowed away in the back of my closet from working in the city. But I'm afraid I'm not much of a dancer."

Bridget laughs and shakes her head. "Well, that makes two of us. I'm trying not to think about that too much."

"We'll get through it," I promise. "So, I guess Millie and Brian are snowed in along with the rest of the East Coast?"

"Unfortunately." She sighs. "So we're gonna need to have a little help to pull this off."

"Okay," I say hesitantly. "What did you have in mind?"

"I think it'll be better to just show you later this afternoon if that's okay? I've got a million things to do to get everything ready, not to mention that Millie and Brian probably won't be back in time to organize the Mistletoe Maze on Sunday. Thankfully we set almost everything up at the Coopers' Tree Farm before they left, but there's still a ton to do on that front too. Since Marie is here to work the front desk this morning I'm going to hide away in the office for a few hours. But I'll come get you for a meeting around three if that works?"

I nod. "Yeah, that's perfect. That's just enough time between lunch and dinner that I'll be able to take a break."

"Sounds good. Thanks again for volunteering to go along with all this," Bridget says genuinely.

"Sure thing. Now, let's get back to work, and I'll see you this afternoon."

CHAPTER 5
BRIDGET

What the hell have I gotten myself into?

After spending the last few hours going through Millie's notes, color swatches, and reference pictures, I have come to the decision that I'm completely in over my head. I've helped plan countless weddings over the years, but never one this size on my own.

Glancing down at the clock, I sigh and stand from my desk. Bessie and Jennie rise from where they've been napping at my feet, and I lean down to pat both their heads.

"I'm gonna leave y'all in here while I go talk to Easton, and I expect you two to be on your best behavior. I mean it, no funny business. Do you hear me?"

The dogs lick my hands in response, and I can't help but giggle at them as I rise to go meet Easton.

Closing the door to my office behind me, I smile at Marie and the new guest she's checking in before heading to the kitchen.

"There's the future Mrs. Morgan," he teases, grinning at

me as I enter. "Give me just a second to finish prepping these fried green tomatoes, and I'm all yours."

I try not to think too hard about how his words make me feel, but I can't deny the butterflies that erupt in my stomach.

"Sounds good," I tell him. Pulling out my phone, I smile at the text from Millie.

Millie: Did you find yourself a groom?

Bridget: Yeah, Easton volunteered this morning.

Millie: Hell yeah.

Millie: I knew it!

Bridget: *eye roll*

Bridget: Sure you did.

Millie: I did! I made a bet with Brian that's who it would be. His guess was Chance, but I knew Easton would beat him to it.

Bridget: Glad you're enjoying this...

Bridget: What's your prize for winning the bet?

Millie: ...

Millie: I'm gonna shield you from that one.

Bridget: I'm gagging. It's fine.

Bridget: This better be the last time I hear about y'all making sex bets that have anything to do with my life.

Millie: :)

Millie: Love you.

Bridget: Love you too.

Tucking my phone back in my pocket, I look up to see Easton drying his hands and smiling over at me.

"Lead the way, wifey," he says, and I giggle as we make our way out of the kitchen.

"Okay, just remember when this meeting is all said and done that you volunteered for this," I tease.

Easton laughs, shrugging his shoulders. "I told you I'm just along for the ride. I'm okay with whatever we need to do to make this happen."

"I'm holding you to that," I say, leading him to the inn's coffee corner where twelve of the town's most notorious busy bodies sit, waiting on us.

"Um, I'm confused," Easton whispers, looking at the group of seventy year old ladies in front of us.

"Just go with it," I whisper, trying not to think too hard about what I'm doing before focusing on the group of women who are all suspiciously quiet.

After a moment, Miss Sally waves her cane in our direction and asks, "Okay, Bridget. What was so important that we had to get out in this cold weather and meet with you. I'm missing my episode of *Wheel of Fortune*."

A few of the ladies nod in agreement, and I try not to cringe as all eyes in the small room look at me expectantly.

"Well, first of all, I really appreciate you all coming," I start. I fidget with my hands nervously until Easton reaches out and grabs one of them, holding it still and nodding at me encouragingly.

I feel the eyes of all the women on us, confident they're clocking every move I make. This part of the plan I concocted with Millie is the part that makes me the most uncomfortable. Along with my hatred for being the center of attention, I despise asking for help. But I know none of this will work without the help of the people in this town.

"We have found ourselves in a little bit of a situation here at Deer Valley," I start. "We had a pretty big wedding scheduled for the weekend, but they're snowed in thanks to the weather."

"Okay, but what does that have to do with us?" Miss Sally asks impatiently, and the ladies around her murmur their agreement.

"Well, I'm getting to that. This wedding has a lot of press. There are several publications coming to do articles on the inn, and it's supposed to be the cover story for a national magazine. We're really counting on the publicity from the article to push us into the next level here at the inn. But since the original wedding is off, we need to pull one together locally in the next two days."

The ladies look between each other, their eyes wide.

"Thankfully, we have most of the big stuff here covered," I continue. "Except the fact that we need these reporters that are coming to believe in this small town love story we're trying to sell them."

"So, wait. Who's getting married, dear?" Miss Ethel asks and the other ladies nod their agreement.

"Easton and I are the bride and groom," I say, and the room erupts into a fit of screams and excited chatter. I give them a moment before holding up my hand to quiet them down.

"I know, I know. But the wedding isn't going to be real. It's all fake, but we've got to make the reporters believe it. Which is where you ladies come in," I finish, looking out at the room.

"This is pretty exciting," Miss Clara squeals, and a few of the other ladies nod their agreement.

"It is," I say with a smile. "But we need to come up with a history on Easton and me, and then I need your help making sure every person in town is on this. Do you think you can help me spread the word?"

All the ladies nod enthusiastically. "We can send it out in the bingo night group chat," one suggests.

"Yes, and I'll send a message to my bookclub and my knitting club," Miss Clara says.

"I'll take care of some of the younger crowd," Miss Sally volunteers. "I'll get Hannah and Caroline to send it out to their friends at school, and Margaret can share the news with anyone who comes into the bakery."

"What's the story going to be though?" Miss Ethel asks. "How did you two meet?"

"Well, I think we should keep it as close to the truth as possible to avoid any confusion. We'll just say we met when he started working at the inn earlier this year, and he proposed sometime last month. It's been a whirlwind romance, but we're completely in love and so excited to start our lives together a little quicker than we planned."

As soon as I'm done talking, the ladies nod, already pulling out their phones to start spreading the latest gossip.

"Thank y'all for your help," I tell them honestly, and they nod before waving us away.

"Well, that wasn't what I expected, but I also think it's kinda brilliant," Easton whispers as we make our way back toward the kitchen. "Those ladies are the biggest gossips I've ever met. It's smart of you to put them to use."

"Thanks," I say. "Sorry again for dragging you into all of this."

"I don't mind a bit," Easton promises. "Now, let's finish planning this wedding."

"HEY EVERYONE. THANK YOU AGAIN FOR ALL YOUR HELP OVER the last few days," I say, looking out at the employees of Deer Valley the following day.

"The inn is a little emptier than normal, thanks to guests being snowed in, but that just means we have more time and attention to devote to the guests that are here," I tell them, and several of the employees nod at me in agreement.

"The reporters will all be here any minute, and I'd just like to remind you all how important these write ups are for us here. We are counting on this publicity to launch us into the new year, and I can't thank you all enough for pitching in to make this a success," I continue before gesturing to Easton.

"And one final reminder that Easton and I are the bride and groom this weekend. As far as the reporters are concerned, we fell in love earlier this year after a whirlwind romance, and he proposed last month in the kitchen here at Deer Valley."

My employees all nod at me, looking between Easton and me curiously. "Does anyone have any questions?"

Everyone shakes their heads, and I nod.

"Perfect. You all know I'm always available to answer any questions you may have or help in any way I can. Between this wedding and the Christmas events coming up next week, I know we're in the midst of busy season around here, but I'm still always here to help."

"Now, let's all get ready to welcome our guests," I finish, smiling out at the group of employees before me.

The crowd disperses, and Easton makes his way over to

me, draping his arm around me. "So, Mrs. Morgan. I have something for you."

I look up at him in confusion, trying to figure out what he's talking about as he pulls a small velvet pink ring box out of his pocket. "I didn't think we could pull this off without this."

My mouth drops open as he opens the box and reveals a beautiful round pink stone surrounded by four smaller diamonds.

"Oh my god, Easton," I gasp. "What on earth is this?"

"Well, I figured we couldn't be fake married without a ring. And I knew pink is your favorite color so when I saw it, I knew you had to have it."

"It's the most beautiful thing I've ever seen, but I can't accept this," I tell him, my eyes wide. "I was planning to just tell them that it was a spontaneous proposal, and we were waiting on it to come in."

"I like my way better," Easton argues, holding out his hand for mine. "It's not really supposed to be a wedding ring, but I remembered I had it stashed away in some of my mom's old jewelry and thought it would be perfect for you."

I place my hand in his, trying to ignore the rush I feel of his hand touching mine. He slips the ring on my finger, and my breath catches at the sight of the sparkling stone on my hand.

"Perfect," he murmurs, dropping a quick kiss to my hand just as the front door of the inn opens.

"Oh my word, you two must be the bride and groom," the woman squeals, looking between Easton and me.

We turn to see a petite, blonde woman rushing into the inn, dragging her suitcase behind her. She hurries over, smiling at us before sticking out her hand to shake mine.

"I'm Catherine Worthington, and I'm the reporter from

Weddings and Wine," she says excitedly, her mouth dropping open as she looks down at my finger.

"Oh my god, I know I'm probably not supposed to say this, but I've worked thousands of weddings in the last few years and this is by far the most beautiful ring I've ever seen," she gushes. "It's so different!"

"Thank you." I smile. "I'm Bridget and this is my fiancé, Easton," I say, trying to ignore how strange the words feel coming from my mouth. "It's so nice to meet you."

"Likewise. I can't believe what a whirlwind this must have been for y'all. How are you feeling?" Catherine asks, looking between the two of us.

"We're just so excited," Easton says, wrapping his arm around me and dropping a kiss to my forehead. "It's not what we were expecting, but I didn't want to wait another day to have her as my wife."

Catherine beams at us, and I immediately know I like her. She's a lot younger than I expected—probably close to my age— and she exudes an excited energy that immediately makes me want to be friends with her.

"Ugh, couples like the two of you are what makes me obsessed with my job," she exclaims, looking between the two of us. I ignore the twinge of guilt that I feel over lying to her, but I remind myself that it's for a good cause as I bury myself closer to Easton's chest.

He smiles down at me and brushes a piece of hair back from my face before turning back to Catherine. "Can I take your bags? I'm sure Bridget wants to give you a tour, but I'd be happy to drop everything off in your room before I have to get back to the restaurant."

"Oh, that would be lovely," Catherine agrees, handing him her luggage before she turns back to me.

"Lead the way, Bridget. I can't wait to hear more about y'all's sweet love story as we walk," she squeals.

I give Easton a nervous look and take a deep breath, preparing myself to put on a show.

I can do this, I remind myself, just as Easton leans in and presses a quick kiss to my lips. I try not to let my surprise show as he winks at me and says, "See you later, Mrs. Morgan."

I smile at him, trying to ignore the way that kiss just turned my world upside down as I lead Catherine through the lobby of the inn. And for the hundredth time in the last few days, I can't help but wonder what the fuck I've gotten myself into.

CHAPTER 6
EASTON

"Can we move the chairs over there to the left?" Bridget asks from where she's standing at the entrance to the vineyard, analyzing the chairs set up in front of her.

"Sure we can," I agree, starting to shift the white folding chairs in the direction she wants. "How's that?"

"Much better," Bridget nods, pulling out her phone. "Ugh, Millie, I love you but I don't have time to talk," she sighs, answering her phone anyway.

"Hey. Yeah, we're a little frantic over here, but we're good. Everything's set up, and the reporters came in this afternoon."

She pauses, listening to whatever Millie is saying on the other end before nodding.

"Yes, we've got it all taken care of. I gave Catherine a tour, and Bobbi and Andy both just got here. I've made sure they're all settled and ready for the festivities in the morning."

She pauses again before rolling her eyes and nodding.

"Yes, I called Miss Cheryl and got her all set up to do my hair and makeup in the morning. I told you, I've got everything handled. Now, you go enjoy the snow and figure out how to get your ass back here in time for the rest of the Christmas festivities this week. I've already talked to the Coopers, and they have everything ready for the Mistletoe Maze. But after that, I really need your help…"

"Perfect, thank you. Yes, I love you too… Okay, bye," Bridget says, sighing as she hangs up the phone. I've just finished moving all the chairs around, so I make my way over to where she's standing and wrap my arm around her.

"Hey, everything's going to be just fine," I promise her. "Everything here looks incredible, and the flowers and the food are all taken care of. The band has confirmed they'll be here tomorrow and the tents are already set up on the other side of the hotel. You've put in the work, and it's going to go perfectly, okay?"

"I still can't believe we're letting Miss Ethel marry us." She sighs, shaking her head. "But since it's not a real wedding, I didn't have any reason to say no when she asked."

"She'll be great," Easton promises. "Now, let's finish getting set up and then we're going home. We need lots of rest before our big day tomorrow."

"I CAN'T BELIEVE WE'RE REALLY DOING THIS," BRIDGET WHISPERS as the photographer snaps the millionth picture of us the following afternoon. We still have a few hours before the wedding, but my cheeks are already sore from smiling.

"Aw, don't tell me you regret it already," I tease. "We haven't even made it down the aisle yet."

"Not even a little bit," she says, looking me up and down. "I've gotta say, you cleaned up pretty good, Mr. Morgan."

"Not as good as you, Mrs. Morgan," I say truthfully. When Bridget first stepped out of the suite upstairs, I have to admit she took my breath away. She looks absolutely perfect in Millie's lace dress, the long sleeves and the cut accentuating her curves perfectly. Combined with the curls in her brown hair, she looks radiant.

"Okay, I think that's all we need," Isabelle, who agreed to step in as the wedding coordinator, says smiling at us as Catherine, Bobbi, and Andy all look on.

"Are there any other shots y'all want us to take?" Bridget asks the reporters and they all shake their heads.

"I think all of those will be perfect," Catherine says. "This is truly the most beautiful venue. And that dress is gorgeous. How in the world did you find that so fast?"

"It was actually Millie's dress first," Bridget admits. "Thankfully, we're the same size, so it worked out perfectly."

"Oh my god, what are the chances of that?" Catherine asks, shaking her head.

"Right, it really was meant to be," Bridget says, smiling up at me, and I lean down to press a kiss to her forehead.

"Y'all are truly a beautiful couple," Bobbi, the reporter for *Southern Weddings* says, and Andy, the reporter for *Bama Brides* nods in agreement.

"Thank you," Bridget says, unable to hide the blush on her cheeks.

Over the last few days, I've become addicted to learning more about Bridget—the way she blushes every time someone pays her the slightest compliment. The way her face lights up when she's talking about something she's excited about. The way she throws her hair on the top of her head while she's stressed.

I remind myself for what feels like the hundredth time that none of this between us is real. Yes, I might be taking advantage of having an excuse to wrap her in my arms and drop quick kisses on her forehead, but by this time tomorrow, all of this will be over.

"Okay, we have about thirty minutes until the guests start to arrive, so let's get you hidden away," Isabelle suggests.

"Sounds good," Bridget agrees, following her toward the inn. "I'll see you at the altar, Easton."

She winks as she heads inside, and I smile at her as she goes.

Her words hit me, and a small part of myself almost wishes that there wasn't anything fake about this wedding. But as soon as I have the thought, I see Miss Ethel and Miss Sally making their way down the slope of the vineyard, heading straight for me.

I take a deep breath as they approach, readying myself for whatever they're about to say.

Miss Sally stops directly in front of me and waves her cane in my face once. "Happy wedding day, Easton," she says, catching me off guard. "I'm happy for you, but next time I think y'all should really plan for something a little easier to get to. These old bones are tired already."

"Yes, ma'am. I only plan to do this once, but I'll let Millie know when she gets back."

Miss Ethel smiles as Miss Sally turns her attention to the reporters. "I don't know you, so you must not be from around here. Who are you?" she asks bluntly, and I fight the urge to cringe at her tone.

"Miss Sally, this is Catherine, Bobbi, and Andy. They're here doing a few features on the inn."

All three of the reporters smile at her warily, and she nods. "Nice to meet you. I'd better get a seat though before they're all gone," Miss Sally says, leaving us to make her way through the crowd.

"And this is Miss Ethel," I say, gesturing to the other woman standing beside me.

Miss Ethel waves before adding, "I'm marrying these two today."

"Oh, it's nice to meet you," Catherine says, immediately coming over to shake Miss Ethel's hand. "Are you so happy for the future Morgans?"

"Positively thrilled," Miss Ethel says before turning to me. "Easton, are you ready to do this?"

"Absolutely," I nod before turning to the reporters. "We're gonna go get set, but we'll see you soon."

They smile at us, waving as we walk away.

As soon as we're out of earshot, Miss Ethel turns to me. "You know, if I didn't know any better, I'd almost think you're looking forward to this."

I smile at her, shrugging my shoulders.

"Miss Ethel, I don't know what you're talking about."

She smirks at me and nods, following me over to where the ceremony is set up. There's already a steady stream of locals pouring in, and I shake my head at how fast all of this came together.

I make small talk with Miss Ethel until Chance walks up, patting me on the shoulder.

"I can't believe you're doing this," he says, shaking his head. "You know, you've only been here a few months. You didn't have to rush in to join all the town chaos at once."

"Well, you know how I feel about being left out," I tease, causing him to roll his eyes at me.

"So, how fake is this thing?" he asks, lowering his voice so that no one else can hear him.

"Well, Miss Ethel is doing the ceremony and unless she got ordained in the last twenty four hours, there's nothing real about it. There's also no marriage license and no official paperwork," I say, and my best friend stares at me for a moment.

"Yeah, I've got that. I know the ceremony is fake but I mean everything else. You actually like her don't you?"

I shrug, trying to decide what to say. "I guess. I mean am I sad for the excuse to spend more time with her? Not at all. But I really am just doing this because she needed help."

"Okay," Chance says. "Whatever you say."

As soon as the words are out of his mouth, music starts to play and Isabelle gestures me over to her.

"Well, it looks like it's time. Good luck," Chance says, patting me on the shoulder.

I make my way over to Isabelle and wait for her to give me the cue to make my way down the aisle. As soon as she nods, I start to walk, and it hits me that I'm really doing this.

Before I know it, I'm standing in front of Miss Ethel, and the crowd turns to focus on Bridget making her way down the aisle.

Even though I already saw her, my breath catches at the sight of her walking down the aisle toward me. She's absolutely breathtaking, and I remind myself again that none of this is real.

As soon as she's close enough to me, I reach out and take her hand. She smiles at me, and I try to focus on whatever Miss Ethel is saying but instead I find myself lost in thought, wishing this wedding wasn't as fake as it actually is.

CHAPTER 7
BRIDGET

"I, Bridget Smith, take you, Easton Morgan, to be my husband. To have and to hold, from this day forward, as long as we both shall live," I finish, smiling at Easton.

The ceremony has passed in a blur, and as soon as I say the words, Miss Ethel is holding out her hand for the rings.

"Easton, please repeat after me. I give you this ring as a symbol of my love and commitment," Miss Ethel says.

Easton repeats the words and slides the thin wedding band onto my hand. My fingers shake at the sight of both it and the engagement band on my finger.

"Now, Bridget, it's your turn. Repeat after me. I give you this ring as a symbol of my love and commitment."

I repeat the words, sliding the gold band I bought for the occasion onto Easton's hand.

"Well, ladies and gentleman, I now pronounce you husband and wife. Easton, you may kiss your bride."

Easton smiles as he leans in and gently grabs my face before dropping a slow kiss onto my lips. I'm vaguely aware of the crowd cheering around us, but really, I'm lost in the way my pretend husband kisses me like there's no tomorrow. Finally, after a minute, he pulls back before dropping a quick kiss to my forehead.

"Come on, Mrs. Morgan. We have a wedding to celebrate."

I let him lead me down the aisle, pausing every few feet to dip me and drop slow kisses to my lips as the guests cheer around us. I make eye contact with Catherine, and she smiles at me from her seat in the back as she jots down something in a small notebook.

"I can't believe we just did that," I whisper, and Easton chuckles as he leads me over to the other side of the inn where the reception is set up.

"I can't either," Easton agrees, grabbing two glasses of champagne from the entryway. "I know it's all for the reporters, but I've gotta say, that felt way more real than I thought it would."

"Uh, yeah. That's an understatement," I say, taking a large sip of my drink.

"Now the fun part, right?" Easton asks, and I smile at his enthusiasm.

"That's right. But I definitely wish we had time to take some dance lessons," I tease, trying not to think about the fact that we'll have to dance in front of the entire town later tonight.

"Oh, we'll be fine. Just follow my lead," he tells me, pulling me into his arms as the guests start to trickle into the tent.

"Whatever you say. I just can't believe how perfect the weather ended up being today," I say, taking another sip of my drink. "Millie and Brian are snowed in, and here we are with sixty-degree weather."

"Yeah, isn't that wild? Hopefully this warm front will make its way toward the city so they can get back home."

"They better," I say, shaking my head. There's no way I can put on all of these holiday events by myself too. Thankfully, we're ahead with the Mistletoe Maze tomorrow, so I feel pretty good about it. And then the cookie celebration is something people do at their own homes on Monday, so there isn't any real planning there except for the competition portion Tuesday night. But if she's not back by Tuesday for Sledding with Santa, I'm going to get her."

Easton laughs, shaking his head. "Well, hopefully it won't come to that. But you sure as hell managed to pull this one off. Really, Bridget, this whole thing is incredible," he says gesturing to the tent in front of us.

I take a minute to take in everything I pulled together in the last three days. Yes, a lot of it was already planned, but I was still responsible for organizing it. And as I look at the huge white floral arrangements and the crowd of locals snacking on the hors d'oeuvres, I can't help but feel a rush of pride.

"You're right," I agree just as Catherine rushes up to us.

"Okay, I've gotta admit when I heard there was a major wedding venue taking over in the middle of nowhere Alabama, I had my doubts. But this wedding is absolutely gorgeous. The scenery with the vineyard in the background? And the color scheme? Most of the time weddings this time of year are all red and green everything, but I love the pops of pink y'all threw in along with the traditional holiday colors. And all the white florals in here along with the floral photo wall? It's perfect," she gushes, causing me to smile.

"Thank you. The photo wall is my favorite too," I say, as the band starts to play.

"Oh, it looks like it's time for our first dance, but please, have something to eat and grab and drink," I encourage her as I let Easton lead me over to the dance floor.

We'd briefly discussed a fun entrance, but seeing that neither of us wanted any more attention than necessary, it felt right for us to just go into our first dance.

The band starts to play "Can't Help Falling in Love with You," and I try to ignore the rush of nerves I feel as Easton leads me to the middle of the floor. The guests around us fall silent, watching as Easton keeps his promise and leads me in a slow dance.

I lose myself in the moment, determined to only focus on the man in front of me and tuning out the rest of the crowd as he spins me around.

The song builds, and Easton dips me, before pulling me close to his body and dropping a kiss to my lips.

Immediately, the same rush hits my veins at the feeling of his mouth on mine, and I kiss him back.

It takes a moment before the cheers of the crowd reach my ears, but as soon as they do, I remember where we are and pull back, my cheeks pink.

Easton grins at my embarrassed expression and I shake my head as I turn to face the crowd of locals.

Just a few more hours.

Otherwise I might get way too comfortable playing the role of Easton Morgan's wife.

"OKAY, I STILL CAN'T BELIEVE WE PULLED THAT OFF," I LAUGH, letting Easton lead me into the honeymoon suite at Deer Valley. We'd briefly debated where we should stay tonight, but we'd ultimately decided that this makes the most sense for our story. After all, the reporters will all be leaving in the morning, and then this whole charade comes to an end.

I try to ignore the pang in my chest at the thought, but the truth is, if today proved anything, it's that I have a major thing for Easton Morgan. I've never met someone that I clicked with so easily, and while at first, I chalked up the rush I felt every time he kissed me today to the fact that it's been a while since I was with someone, I can't pretend that I don't love how his mouth feels on mine.

"There's no we to it. You did all of that," Easton insists.

"Pretty sure I couldn't marry myself." I laugh. "That makes you a pretty important part of the equation."

"Yeah, yeah," Easton says, brushing me off. I turn to unlock the door, holding it open for him to enter and following behind him.

As we enter the room, I freeze.

How in the hell did I overlook the fact that there's definitely two of us and only one bed in this room?

Easton walks over to the desk where Isabelle sat our bags, grabbing a pair of pajamas out and looking up to find me still frozen in the doorway.

"Bridget, what's wrong?" he asks, the concern evident in his voice.

"Uh, I'm an idiot. I forgot there was one bed when we made this plan. I'm so sorry, Easton. I feel so silly," I babble, worried he's going to feel uncomfortable with the thought of sharing a bed with me. "I can go stay in another room."

"Bridget, calm down," Easton says, walking over and wrapping his arm around me. "You know, I kind of assumed the honeymoon suite would only have one bed. And you can't stay anywhere else. What if the reporters see us leaving different rooms? Then all of this work would have been for nothing."

I pause, realizing he's right. Blowing out a sigh, I steady myself and nod at him. "Okay fine. But I already pushed you into this crazy scheme. I just don't want you to feel uncomfortable."

"Bridget, you haven't pushed me into anything. If you're really uncomfortable, I'll sleep on the floor if I need to. But I'm good with this."

"You're not sleeping on the floor," I insist, shaking my head at him. "We're both adults. There's no reason we can't sleep in the same bed."

"Are you sure?" Easton asks, and I nod.

"Positive," I promise him. "Honestly, I just need to get out of this dress, and I'll be a happy girl."

My cheeks heat at the way that sounded, and Easton chuckles. "I feel the same way about this tux. I'm gonna go change and grab a quick shower, but I'll knock before I come back in so you can get changed."

"Sounds good," I say, waiting for him to leave before reaching back to try to unzip my dress. I twist myself to the left and to the right, determined to get out of the dress on my own. I spend a few more minutes reaching this way and that, doing everything I can to lower the zipper of the damned dress. Eventually, by the time I hear the shower cut off, I'm covered in a light sheen of sweat from my efforts and I'm forced to admit defeat.

"Uh, Easton?" I call out, burying my face in my hands.

"What's up?" he calls back through the door.

"Do you think you can unzip my dress?" I ask.

"Sure, give me just a second. I need to get dressed," he responds, and it's all I can do to not think too hard about the fact that he's naked on the other side of that door.

Finally, after what feels like forever, he emerges from the bathroom, a cloud of steam following him as he makes his way over to me.

"Turn around for me, Sugar," he instructs, and I smile at the sound of the nickname falling from his lips.

"It looks like you managed to get the zipper stuck in the lining," he says, looking at the back of my dress. "Just give me a second."

I nod and try to ignore the feeling of his warm hands on my back while he fiddles with the zipper. After a few minutes, he manages to free the lining, and starts to unzip the dress, leaving my back bare until the zipper reaches the lace of my pink panties.

His fingers brush against the lace, and I let out a small groan as his hands brush against my ass.

Immediately, my cheeks heat and I rush to grab my clothes, while trying to make sure I keep the top of my dress covering myself.

"I'll be back," I squeak, basically running into the bathroom and slamming the door behind me.

God, what the hell is wrong with me?

Taking a deep breath, I step out of the dress and hang it on the ledge of the door before reaching up to free the bobby pins from my hair. By the time I step into the shower, I've managed to calm myself down, and I take my time washing my hair over and over, trying to get all the product out of it.

Finally, after the fourth wash, I give up, rinsing my hair and stepping out of the shower.

As I get dressed, I remind myself that all of this will be over tomorrow, and I sigh, trying to decide how I feel about that.

Walking out into the bedroom, I smile at the sight of Easton already asleep on the bed in front of me. I turn the light off and crawl into bed, trying to be careful not to disturb him.

But as I close my eyes, he rolls over and pulls my body to his, wrapping me in his arms as he sleeps peacefully beside me.

Yeah, this I could definitely get used to.

CHAPTER 8
EASTON

"Are you ready to send these reporters on their way?" I ask as I step out of the bathroom the following morning. Bridget is fully dressed, and she toys with her hair in the mirror over the desk before sighing.

"Yeah, let's get this over with," she says. "I don't think I'm ever going to get all the product Miss Cheryl put in my hair yesterday out. I washed it four times, and it still feels like there's a whole bottle of hairspray in there."

"You look great," I tell her honestly, trying not to stare at how true that is. "Now, let's get these reporters out of here, wifey."

Bridget laughs, checking her hair one more time before leading me out of the room and into the lobby.

As soon as we enter the large room, I catch sight of the three reporters standing in front of the Christmas tree, chatting.

"Good morning," Bridget says cheerfully, smiling at the three of them.

"Good morning," they all respond.

"Bridget, I've got to say, you really have something special here," Bobbi says, gesturing around the inn. "I know we're all about the weddings, but I've already told my husband that we have to plan a trip here sometime soon."

Bridget nods enthusiastically. "Of course. We'd love to have you any time."

"I'll make a reservation for later next year," Bobbi promises."And we'll be in touch if we need anything else for the article."

"Sounds perfect," Bridget says, waving as Bobbi heads out the front door.

"Thank y'all so much again," Bridget says, smiling at the two remaining reporters. "We're so happy you chose to stay with us."

Andy nods. "Well, I've got to get going, but I really enjoyed it. Thank you for letting us be a part of your special day."

She makes her way out of the inn, leaving us standing with Catherine. Bridget reaches out to pull her into a hug, and Catherine smiles widely.

"So, I've got to say, I've just absolutely fallen in love with this little town. And I was thinking, since y'all seem to have some rooms open from the wedding that was canceled, would it be possible for me to just stay?"

Bridget and I both freeze at her question. "Stay?" Bridget chokes out, trying to keep her composure. "Like stay at Deer Valley?"

"Yeah, that's kind of what I was thinking. If not, I totally get it, but I don't really have anyone to celebrate Christmas with, and I heard so much about the different events coming up I just thought it might be fun. Obviously, I'll pay for my room and everything. To be honest, I'm just not quite ready to leave."

"Oh, sure," Bridget says hesitantly. "How long are you thinking?"

"Through the twenty-sixth of its possible," Catherine says, and Bridget squeezes my hand as she tries to hide her panic.

"Um, sure, I think we can make that happen," I say, trying to calm Bridget down.

"Oh, I'm just so excited," Catherine cheers. "Well, I'm sure I'll be seeing you two lovebirds all over the place. I can't wait to spend more time together."

With that, she turns and heads back to the elevator, leaving me there with a completely panicked Bridget.

"Looks like we're not done playing husband and wife." I laugh, wrapping my arm around her. "Let's get out of here and we'll come up with a plan."

"Everything's going to be totally fine," I promise Bridget, leading her into the Mistletoe Maze the following night. "We got Miss Ethel and Miss Sally to get the word out that Catherine is staying in town, and I'm staying at your house for the next few days just to be safe. Now, you worked your tail off over the last few weeks to make sure this event goes well, and I'm really looking forward to seeing what this Mistletoe Maze is all about. So take a deep breath and let's do this."

My words must be enough to pull Bridget from the trance she was in because she straightens her shoulders and nods, looking determined.

"You're right," she agrees. "And I think you're going to love this tradition. It really is one of my favorites."

I follow her through the entrance to the Christmas tree farm, shaking my head at the sheer number of lights in front of us. Almost every tree in the farm is covered in Christmas lights, and above the trees, there's also strings of lights illuminating the path.

"It's beautiful," I say truthfully, a little awestruck by the sheer number of lights surrounding us.

"Yeah, the Coopers are pretty incredible, and they plant the trees in different patterns every year. We rotate the part of the field that we use, and then we put up the lights to make it feel a little more festive and light the way."

"Where does the mistletoe come in?" I ask.

Bridget laughs before pointing to the rows of mistletoe above our heads.

"Oh, makes sense." I laugh, grabbing her hand and pulling her toward me before leaning down and dropping a kiss on her forehead.

"Aww, aren't y'all the sweetest," a voice says from behind us, and I turn to see Miss Ethel and Miss Sally watching us.

"Oh, well, just keeping up the charade, you know?" Bridget says quickly. "Catherine is here somewhere, remember?"

"Right," Miss Sally says skeptically.

"Sure thing, dear. Whatever you say." Miss Ethel laughs.

I want to tell Bridget that Catherine was the furthest thing from my mind when I kissed her, but I push it away, knowing now isn't the right time for that conversation.

"There you two are," Catherine yells, spotting us through the crowd. "Bridget, this is absolutely incredible," she says, gesturing to the scene in front of us. "This town is just so pleasantly full of surprises."

"I'm glad you're enjoying yourself," Bridget says with a smile.

"Absolutely," Catherine agrees. "I've been so productive over the last few days too. I swear, there's some magic in this little place."

I think about it for a moment, silently agreeing with her. This situation with Bridget and me would have probably never happened in the city, and it makes me pause. I know this thing between us isn't real, but combined with the way I already felt about her, the last few days have been a picture into what Bridget and I could have between us.

Am I ready to give this up on the twenty-sixth? I ask myself and as soon as the thought crosses my mind, I know the answer is no.

But can I convince her that what we have is real? That I'm not so sure about. Sighing, I look down at her, filled with a new determination to make this thing between us work.

I guess it's time to see just how magical this time of year really is.

CHAPTER 9
BRIDGET

"Good morning, Sugar," Easton says as I step into the kitchen the next morning,

"Good morning. Is this coffee fresh?" I ask, grabbing a coffee cup out of the cabinet.

"Sure is," he tells me, opening the fridge and grabbing my favorite gingerbread creamer. "Here you go."

"Thanks," I smile, busying myself with fixing my coffee. Bringing the cup to my lips, I take a long sip and sigh happily at the taste of the sweet liquid hitting my tongue.

"Good?" Easton asks, smiling over at me.

"Perfect," I answer, taking another sip. "So, what do you have planned for today?"

"Well, I was about to cook some breakfast, and then I need to go into Deer Valley for a few hours. I know Greta is kind of covering everything this week, but I just want to make sure she's not overwhelmed. And when I get home, I figured we could bake our cookies for the celebration if you'd like."

"That sounds perfect," I agree. "I've got a few admin tasks

I need to take care of in the office, and then a few final things to wrap up before Brian and Millie come home tomorrow."

"Sounds good. But first, we're gonna have breakfast together," Easton says, pulling a loaf of bread off the top of the fridge.

"Oh, you don't have to do that," I say, not wanting him to feel like he needs to take care of me.

"I know I don't, but I want to," he says, smiling at me as he starts to pull things from the fridge. "Plus, I'm pretty sure I promised you some eggnog french toast earlier this week."

"You did, didn't you?" I laugh, sitting down at the counter and pulling my laptop out of my bag.

"What are you working on?" Easton asks curiously as he gets to work on breakfast.

"Oh, just making sure all our invoices are paid for the events over the next few days," I answer, going back through my emails to confirm that I haven't missed anything.

"You know, you work harder than anyone I know," Easton says seriously. "Do you ever take a break?"

"Um, I'm not great at breaks," I admit honestly.

"When's the last time you took an actual vacation?" Easton asks, looking at me suspiciously. "And I'm not talking about taking the day to catch up on work at home or spending the day sick in bed. I mean an actual planned vacation."

I blink at him, trying to think about the answer to his question and coming up empty. "Uh, I guess it has been a little while," I admit. "But we've been so busy with everything at Deer Valley, there hasn't been a good time. And I'm lucky enough that I really love my job, so I don't mind."

"Well, I'm glad to hear that you love your job, but I still think you need to take a break, Sugar. Promise me, after this is all over, you'll schedule some time to go do something fun."

I look over at him, smiling at the serious look on his face as he dips the bread in the French toast mixture beside the stove.

"I'll see what I can do," I promise. "But you're really one to talk. Since you started earlier this year, I'm pretty sure you haven't missed a single day of work either."

"Fine, I'll give you that," Easton says with a laugh just as Bessie and Jennie come running out of the bedroom, obviously excited by the smells coming from the kitchen.

"Whoa, girlies, slow it down," I say with a laugh, shaking my head as they sit at Easton's feet, waiting for him to give them a piece of what he's cooking. Shaking his head, he drops a piece of crust from the bread for both dogs, and the sound of their tails slapping the hardwood floor fills the room as they munch away happily.

"All right, I've fed you girls, now it's time to feed your momma." Easton laughs, and the dogs look up at me expectantly.

I smile at the words and try to take a moment to remind myself that this isn't my real life. With us temporarily living together and putting on the facade of being a happily married couple, it's too easy to forget that none of this is real.

"You okay?" Easton asks as he slides a plate in front of me, and I pull myself from the direction my thoughts were heading.

I nod before looking down at the food. "Oh my god, Easton, this smells incredible," I tell him, soaking in the sweet scent of the breakfast in front of me.

I take a small bite and let out a moan at the sugary breakfast. "Okay, I completely get the hype now," I admit, and Easton winks at me.

"Damn, Sugar. You sure are good for my ego. I've never had a girl moan for me that easily," he teases, shooting me a wink as he places another piece of bread on the skillet in front of him.

My face heats in embarrassment, causing Easton to laugh.

"I'm sorry, I'm just teasing," he says as I take another bite of my food. "But I've gotta say, you're so pretty when you blush."

I smile, unsure of what to say as he slides his toast onto his plate and comes to sit next to me. We eat in comfortable silence, and I can't help but think I could really get used to spending my mornings with Easton Morgan.

"ARE YOU READY TO DOMINATE THIS COOKIE CELEBRATION?" I ask as I pull the canisters of flour and sugar out of the cabinet.

"Um, I don't know about dominating, but we'll see what we can do," Easton says with a laugh.

I look at him and roll my eyes. "Easton, you're a chef at the most popular restaurant in town. There's no way we're not winning this thing."

"Um, Bridget, I hate to break it to you, but I'm not a pastry chef. And Margaret, the owner of the bakery, is entering too. She's been planning her entries for weeks."

"Okay, well, that may be true. But we're still gonna give her a run for her money," I insist. "Now, grab the butter and eggs out of the fridge, and let's get started."

"Anything for you, wifey," he teases, moving over to the fridge to grab the rest of the ingredients.

I pull the mixer down out of the cabinet, and start to add in the butter, eggs and sugar. We make quick work of mixing the dough together, and I sprinkle some flour on the counter as Easton grabs the rolling pin and the cookie cutters out of the drawer.

Just as I turn to pick up the mixing bowl, something hits the side of my face, and I let out a squeal. Wiping my cheek, I look down at my fingers that are now covered in flour before turning to stare at Easton in shock.

"Did you really just throw flour at me?" I ask, glancing down at his flour covered fingers.

"Sure did, Sugar," he says, smiling mischievously at me.

"I'm going to get you back," I promise. "But I'm gonna wait til you're least expecting it."

"Whatever you say." Easton laughs as I transfer the dough over to the counter.

"So, are you regretting this whole setup yet?" I ask, grabbing the rolling pin from where Easton left it sitting on the counter.

"Not even a little bit," Easton says, and I feel the familiar tug in my stomach at the words. "What about you?"

"I can't say I have any complaints," I admit, starting to roll out the dough.

"Here, let me do that," Easton insists, and his arm brushes against mine as he moves to help me. I tell myself that I need to move, but I feel frozen in place, soaking in the feeling of having him this close to me. He looks down at me before reaching to touch my face.

"Sorry, you still have some flour on you," he murmurs, and I revel in the feeling of his hot breath against my face. Without thinking, I tilt my face closer to his, and our lips graze.

I let out a sigh of contentment, and Easton claims my

mouth, kissing me hard. I reach up and thread my fingers through his hair just as the buzzer of the oven goes off. We jump apart as if we've been electrocuted, and I can't help the laugh that bubbles out of me.

"Uh, well, it looks like the oven is preheated. We'd better get the first batch in. And once we do that, we should probably start on the icing, don't you think? I'm thinking we do the Santa cookies first, if that sounds okay with you. Then we can work on the stockings," I babble, trying not to focus on how good his lips felt on mine.

"Yeah, that sounds good, Sugar," Easton agrees, smiling down at me before turning back to continue rolling out the dough.

We work quietly, cutting out the cookies and sitting them on the sheet.

"Okay, set us a timer for ten minutes, and we'll whip up the icing while we wait," Easton suggests as he slides the sheet into the oven.

"Sounds good," I agree, pulling out my phone and setting the timer before turning back to Easton.

He's grabbing the powdered sugar out of my pantry, and I try to ignore how good he looks in the dark green flannel he's wearing.

"So, do you think Catherine is enjoying her stay?" Easton asks, pulling me from my thoughts.

"Yeah, I talked to her last night at the maze, and she seemed really excited about the rest of the activities," I tell him, and he nods.

"I think you should be really proud of everything you've managed to pull together," Easton says, and I look over at him in surprise.

"Oh, I don't know about that," I say hesitantly. "None of it would have been possible without you and the rest of the staff at Deer Valley. Plus, Millie did a lot of the work before she left so I can't take credit for that either."

"Bridget, when are you going to stop selling yourself short?" Easton asks. "Everyone at the inn knows how hard you work. With how busy Brian stays handling everything with the town, there's no way he and Millie could keep that place open without you running everything. The employees all adore you, and there's no one else in that place that could've pulled off everything you have in the last week."

I blink, trying to decide if he's serious. Realizing he is, I feel the blush fill my cheeks as I focus on mixing the icing.

"I don't know about all that," I say hesitantly. "But thank you. I definitely couldn't have done it without you."

"Sure thing, Sugar," Easton teases.

"Why have you started calling me Sugar?" I ask curiously.

Easton moves closer, placing his arms on either side of the counter beside me, caging me in. I suck in a sharp breath, surprised at feeling him so close.

"Because, Sugar, there's nothing in this kitchen that tastes as sweet as you do, " he whispers, nuzzling his face against my neck. I sigh at the feeling of his coarse beard hair rubbing against my neck as I reach over and turn the mixer off.

"Oh," I say simply, my mind completely blank as I try to decide how to respond to that.

"Yeah, oh," he murmurs, turning me to face them. "And I've gotta be honest, I'm dying for another taste."

As soon as the words are out of his mouth, he leans in and presses his lips to mine, kissing me hard.

I lose myself immediately in the feeling of his mouth against mine, pulling him closer. His body presses mine against the counter, and I resist the urge to roll my hips against his.

"So damn sweet," he whispers, running his tongue down the curve of my neck.

"Easton," I gasp, pulling him closer and bringing his mouth back to mine.

"I know, Sugar," he murmurs, tracing his fingers under my sweater. "I've been going crazy thinking about tasting the rest of you, but I'm not moving forward with anything more until you beg."

His words light a fire inside my veins, and I find myself nodding. "Please, Easton," I beg. "Whatever you want, it's yours."

He groans at my words before tugging my sweater over my head. "God, I love the sound of that."

He continues to kiss me, lifting me from where I'm standing and setting me on the counter beside the mixer. Without thinking, I reach down and stick my fingers in the mixer and dab a small bit of icing on his cheek. He pulls back, looking at me in shock before starting to laugh.

"Oh, Bridget," he whispers, wiping the icing from his face and sucking it into his mouth. "You're always full of surprises. But as good as that tastes, I'd still rather have you against my tongue."

He leans in and pulls his mouth back to mine, threading his fingers through my hair.

Suddenly, it's like a fire's lit between the two of us, both of us desperate to feel each other's hands everywhere. His hands reach up to tug down my bra as mine reach for the buckle on his belt.

"Sugar, this one isn't about me," he whispers, dropping his mouth to my chest and sucking my nipple into his mouth.

I moan at the sensation as he sucks and bites before he pulls back and grins. "So fucking sweet."

Reaching down, I pull his shirt over his head and groan at the sight of his muscular chest. I lose myself in admiring his bare chest for a moment, just as the alarm goes off for the cookies.

"Fuck," he whispers. "I'm tempted to let those cookies burn so I can stay right here."

"I'll get them," I volunteer, climbing down from my spot on the counter. Easton moves back and leans against the counter, crossing his arms and smiling as I prance across the kitchen.

Leaning down, I pull the sheet pan out of the oven and place the hot cookies on top of the stove.

As soon as I shut the oven door, I feel Easton behind me, and I smile as he scoops me back up into his arms before sitting me back on the counter.

"I'm not anywhere close to being done with you," he whispers, pulling his mouth back to mine.

We kiss for a few minutes, and I groan as his hands wander down to my leggings. He pulls me closer, helping me wiggle free of the fabric, leaving me sitting in front of him in just my lacy panties.

"Damn it, Sugar," he moans, and I blush at the feeling of his eyes raking over me. I start to wrap my arms around myself, suddenly feeling extremely self conscious.

Easton gives me a look, grabbing my hands and pulling them away from my stomach, taking me all in. "Now, Bridget, I'm not going to rush push you into anything you aren't ready for, but I'm also not going to let you sit here and act like you're not the most beautiful thing I've ever seen."

I blink at him, trying to decide what to say as he leans down and kisses me again. After a moment, he pulls back and looks at me seriously. "Tell me, do you want to stop?"

I shake my head immediately, trying to figure out what to

say. "I'm sorry, I don't want to stop. It's just been a long time since I've done this, and I guess I'm feeling a little nervous," I admit, hating the way I feel my face flush with embarrassment.

"There's no rush," Easton says gently. "I just want to make you feel good."

"I want that too," I whisper truthfully, and Easton smiles.

"Good, Sugar, because there's something else I'm dying to taste."

I freeze, the mixture of warmth at his words and the rush of nerves filling my chest. But nothing is stronger than the overwhelming desire to finally give in to what's been building between us.

Easton smirks as he sinks down to his knees, and I groan at the sight of him below me. He leans in to press a kiss to my panties, and I let out a squeak of surprise at feeling his lips on me.

"Something tells me this is gonna be the sweetest fucking thing yet," he whispers, sliding my panties to the side before he leans in to taste me.

"Oh my god," I moan, scooting my hips down to wrap my legs around his neck and rolling my hips against his mouth. He continues to lick and suck on my clit before he reaches up to slide one finger inside me.

"So fucking sweet," he whispers sounding almost reverent as I lie back against the cabinets behind me and use my legs to pull him closer.

"Easton," I groan.

"I know," he groans, continuing to tease and suck at my clit while his finger slides in and out of me. "Such a perfect pussy. Now, I want to feel my wife come on my tongue. Can you do that for me, Sugar?"

I moan in agreement, rolling my hips faster against his

face as I feel my orgasm start to build. It briefly crosses my mind that I've never come this fast in my life, but I'm immediately distracted by the feeling of his mouth against me. "Don't stop," I beg, relishing the feeling of his beard rubbing against the sensitive skin on the inside of my thighs.

"Wouldn't dream of it," he promises, adding another finger as he slides it in and out of my pussy, making me groan.

"I'm close," I whimper, at the same time as he clamps his mouth down against my clit. "Holy shit, yes."

I tighten my legs around his face as my orgasm tears through me, hitting me hard and fast. Easton's mouth continues to work against my clit, making my orgasm feel like it's never going to end.

Finally, after what feels like forever, my orgasm starts to slow, and I smile down at him. He pulls back, freeing his fingers from my pussy before sucking them into his mouth.

"I was right, Sugar. So fucking sweet," he says with a wink. Now, let's get dressed. We've got a competition to win."

CHAPTER 10
EASTON

think our cookies turned out pretty good," Bridget says, looking down at the large tray of cookies we finished late last night.

"I think so too," I agree, my mind immediately going back to how fucking incredible it felt to taste her. I couldn't sleep last night, my mind completely filled with dread at the idea of losing this feeling in just a few days. Agreeing to marry Bridget was the best idea I've ever had, and I have to admit, I become a little more obsessed with her each day.

"Hey, what's on your mind?" Bridget asks, looking at me from where she's working on her computer.

"I've been thinking, and I have a proposal." I admit.

She looks at me expectantly, and I decide to go for it before I lose my nerve. "We clearly have a lot to figure out, but I propose that, at least through Christmas, we see where this thing goes between us. I really like you, Bridget. And after last night, I think you might like me too."

"I do," she admits. "But how will this work after Catherine leaves? I know we're putting on a pretty convincing show, but in case you forgot, we're not married in real life."

"I know," I say, taking a deep breath. "We'll figure all of that out later, but for now, what do you say to just seeing where this goes?"

"I kinda like the idea," Bridget admits. "What about the town though? What will they think?"

"Well, first of all, I don't really give a shit," I say with a laugh. "But even if we did, we have the fake wedding as an excuse for a few more days."

"That's true," Bridget says, looking at me excitedly. "I say let's do it, then."

I smile at her, pulling her into my arms and dropping a kiss to her lips. "Music to my ears, Sugar."

"I CAN'T BELIEVE WE PLACED SECOND," BRIDGET POUTS, crossing her arms over her chest.

"Well, I know it's disappointing, but did you see those cookies that Margaret made? The reindeer were all connected to the sleigh, and they moved. Plus, they were the best sugar cookie I've ever tasted," I say, and Bridget laughs.

"Okay, fine. You're right. That was pretty darn cool," Bridget agrees. "I bet we could have won if we hadn't had to spend so much time remaking everything after our little escapades."

I shrug. "Sorry, there's some parts of food safety that I take seriously."

Bridget giggles, shaking her head at me. "Aren't you a

good little chef," she teases. "But mark my words, we're going for the win in the sweater competition tomorrow."

"Whatever you say," I agree, nodding at her.

"And on the plus side, Millie and Brian are finally back in town so they'll be able to put together most of the other events without me."

"That's definitely a plus. I think you've earned yourself a break, Mrs. Morgan."

"I don't know about a break." She laughs. "But I'll agree to just slowing down a little bit."

"I'll take it," I concede, knowing that's the best she'll give me.

"So, what do you think of this event?" Bridget asks, gesturing to the Sledding with Santa event that's currently ongoing.

"It's another fun one," I agree, looking up at the hill that's covered in fake snow. The children and parents zip up and down the hill while families take turns visiting the Santa station that's set up at the base of the hill.

"Yeah, I wish we'd had this when I was a kid." Bridget laughs. "But knowing how clumsy I can be, it's probably a good thing we didn't."

I laugh, shaking my head at her. "Yeah, you're probably right," I agree. "After seeing you trying to walk the dogs this morning, I don't know if I can argue with you there."

Bridget sticks her tongue out at me, rolling her eyes. "Bessie and Jennie completely tripped me. It's not my fault!"

"Sure, I'm sure it's all their fault," I tease.

"There's the blushing bride," someone squeals, and we turn to see Millie sprinting in our direction before she almost tackles Bridget in a hug.

"Yeah, pretty sure neither of you need to get anywhere

close to that slope," Brian mumbles under his breath, and I nod in agreement.

"Thank god you're finally back," Bridget says, hugging Millie tight to her chest. "I want to hear all about New York."

"It looks like we both have a lot to catch up on, huh?" Millie asks, looking between Bridget and me suspiciously. "How's the happy couple?"

"We're great," I answer, sliding my arm around Bridget and tugging her to my side.

Millie and Brian's eyes both widen in surprise as they look between us. "What's going on here?" Brian asks.

"We're still figuring that out," I admit, and Millie lets out an excited little shriek.

"I knew it," she yells excitedly, pulling Bridget from my arms and wrapping her arms around her. "Brian, I totally won the bet."

"Millie, what did I tell you about making bets with my cousin about my love life?" Bridget sighs, and I laugh, dropping a kiss to her forehead.

CHAPTER 11
BRIDGET

"Okay, we may have come in second in the cookie competition, but I'm determined to take first with these sweaters," I tell Easton, pulling the rolls of multicolored ribbon I bought out of the bag.

"I agree," Easton says, looking down at the piles of fabric, pipe cleaners, tinsel, and bows I already poured on the floor in front of us. "Did you leave anything for the rest of the town to buy or is that part of your strategy?"

"Well, I wasn't sure what direction we were planning to go in, so I just grabbed a bit of everything," I say with a laugh, realizing I might have gone a little overboard as I look at the pile in front of us.

"That's fair. So what are you thinking about doing?" Easton asks, pulling the oversized sweatshirts I grabbed for us out of the bag.

"Well, I figured these sweatshirts would be easier to attach everything to, plus they were cheaper than buying a plain sweater just to cover it with all this shit. So that's about as far as I've made it. But I did think we could do something super cheesy like 'Tying the Knot this Christmas' and then just cover the whole thing with bows and tinsel."

Easton nods slowly, taking in everything in front of him. "I like it. But I think we need a few more Christmas elements if we want to win this thing."

"Yeah, you're right," I agree, wracking my brain for a way to make the sweaters more festive.

"Let's just start with making some bows and we'll go from there," Easton suggests, and I nod, grabbing the lime green ribbon that caught my eye in the store.

"So I saw this new method for the really big bows, but I think it's going to require two people," I tell him, unwrapping the ribbon and pulling some of it free from the spool.

"No problem. Just tell me what to do," Easton says, and I sit on the floor and start winding the ribbon around my fingers.

Easton sits beside me and watches as I fumble with the ribbon, pulling it every which way until eventually it ends up wrapped around my hands, binding them together in front of me.

"I definitely did something wrong," I groan, looking over to Easton and realizing his eyes are blazing as he looks at me.

"Damn, you look so pretty all tied up," he growls, and my breath catches in my throat at the change in his tone.

"I want to see you tied up like this for me without all the clothes," Easton mumbles.

I nod enthusiastically. I haven't been able to stop thinking about the way that his hands and tongue felt on me the other day, and the idea of having him that way again immediately has heat rushing to my core.

"Yes, please," I murmur, pulling my hands free from the ribbon and reaching to strip his shirt off of him.

Immediately, his hands drift to my waist, tugging my shirt over my head, and I groan as the cool air hits my chest.

"So fucking perfect," Easton mumbles, stepping back to admire the way I look in my red lacy bra and leggings. I feel my cheeks heat the same way they always do as he attempts to admire me, but he gives me a knowing wink as reaches back to unclasp my bra and drops a slow kiss to my mouth.

"This is all I've thought about for the last two days," Easton admits and I can't help the rush I feel at his words.

"Me too," I mumble, desperate to feel him everywhere.

As soon as the words are out of my mouth, Easton's mouth clashes with mine, and I reach out to pull him as close as I can to me. Our tongues tangle, and he nips my bottom lip, making me groan at the sensation.

"Such a sweet girl," he teases, and I pull him back, immediately missing the feeling of his mouth on mine.

"Greedy, greedy," he teases, pushing me back until I'm lying flat on the floor. He follows me down, settling between my thighs as he rests on top of me. I sigh at the feeling of his hard length rubbing against my clit through his sweatpants.

"Damn, you feel good," Easton whispers. "But I think there's still too much clothing between us."

He reaches down and tugs my leggings and panties down my legs, leaving me bare in front of him.

He pulls back, taking me in, and I groan in frustration, missing the feeling of him against me.

"Don't worry, sweetheart, I'm nowhere close to being through with you."

He grabs the ribbon I was struggling with and gently binds my hands with it above my head. The ribbon isn't too tight, but the feeling of knowing I'm bound for him has me feeling desperate. I've never done anything like this in my life, and I realize this is yet another feeling Easton has introduced me to that I could become addicted to.

"Please, Easton," I beg, and he smiles down at me, letting his fingers tease my bare nipples as he takes his time teasing me.

"What do you want, Sugar?" Easton asks. "I want to hear you say it."

"I want you to fuck me, please," I whisper.

"What was that? I couldn't hear you." He smirks, continuing to tease my nipples. I roll my hips, trying to get some friction for the desperate need coursing through me, but it's no use. Without the use of my hands I'm totally at his mercy, and there's nothing I can do to rush this.

"Please, Easton. I want you to fuck me," I say, making sure my words are as clear as possible. "I want to feel your cock inside me."

"Fuck yes," Easton moans. He reaches down to tug off his sweatpants, freeing his cock, and I suck in a breath at the size of him.

"Oh my god, you're huge," I groan, feeling a mixture of desperation to finally have him combined with a slight wave of nerves.

"Damn, you're good for my ego," he teases, reaching down to toy with my clit.

I groan at the sensation, losing myself in the feeling of his hands on me.

He teases me with his fingers, sliding them in and out of me as I whimper and beg for him.

"So fucking wet for me, Sugar," he murmurs, adding another finger inside me.

"Please, Easton," I beg again, and finally he nods, stepping back from me.

I whine at the loss of contact, and he looks down at me,

holding up his hand. "I promise I'll be right back. I'm just going to grab a condom."

"Fuck the condom," I whisper. "I have an IUD, and I need to feel all of you. If you're comfortable with it, of course." I add.

"Completely comfortable with it," he murmurs, walking back to me and teasing my pussy with his cock.

I cry out at the contact, rolling my hips in desperation to get him to finally slide inside me.

"Such a needy girl, aren't you, Sugar," he teases, and I whimper as the tip of his dick starts to slide into my pussy.

"Yes, fuck me, please," I beg, completely lost in him to the point I'm not really even sure what I'm begging for.

Finally, he shifts his hips, letting his cock slide fully inside me, and I groan at the intrusion. "So damn tight," he mutters, letting me adjust to his size before starting to fuck into me.

"Oh my god," I cry, working my hips against him and already feeling my climax starting to build.

"That's right, sweet girl. I can't wait to see my wife dripping with my cum," he mumbles, fucking me hard.

I moan at the sound of the filthy words coming from his mouth.

"Are you gonna be a good girl and come for me?" he asks, reaching down and lightly pinching my clit.

The sensation is enough to tip me over the edge, and I tighten around him, my orgasm tearing through me.

"So. Damn. Good," he groans, moving his hips faster and fucking me harder until I feel him coming inside me.

"God, you're so fucking perfect." He pulls back and lets out a moan at the sight of his cum spilling out of me. "Come on, let me fix you some dinner and then we're doing that again."

"Dinner?" I ask, shaking my head at the turn this moment just took.

"Yeah, I was thinking chicken pesto pasta," he says, as if he didn't just have me begging for his cock a few seconds ago.

"Easton Morgan, what am I going to do with you?" I laugh, shaking my head.

CHAPTER 12
EASTON

"God, this night is just what I needed," Bridget groans, collapsing on the couch the following night and pulling a blanket over her legs. Bessie and Jennie immediately jump in her lap, and she smiles as she reaches to pet them.

"Well, I'd say you've more than earned a night off," I agree. "But it was nice of Millie to insist you stay in tonight."

"Yeah, it was. Especially since we never bothered to finish the sweaters we were supposed to wear tonight," she says, a small blush taking over her cheeks at the memory of how we spent last night.

"I don't have any complaints," I say, sitting down next to her and pulling her into my arms.

She smiles, wrapping her arms around my shoulder before letting out a sigh. "Whatever you're cooking in there smells amazing."

"Thanks. I hope it's edible," I tease, dropping a kiss to her forehead.

"I'm sure it's perfect," Bridget assures me. "What are we having?"

"I just threw together some spinach and cranberry stuffed chicken and some mashed potatoes. The chicken needs about five more minutes in the oven, and then we'll be ready to eat."

"Hmm, a man who gives me orgasms and cocks for me… what more could a girl want?" Bridget teases, and I laugh, lifting her and settling her back on the couch next to her dogs.

"I'll be right back. While I finish dinner, you decide on what movie you want to watch."

Bridget nods, reaching for the remote and flipping through the streaming services as I head into the kitchen.

Grabbing a bottle of wine out of the fridge, I pour us both a glass before taking the chicken out of the oven. Plating it and the potatoes quickly, I carry Bridget's food into the living room, handing her the wine and the plate.

"Oh my god," Bridget groans. "I'm totally gonna be spoiled after this."

I smile as she takes a sip of her wine and starts to eat before I head back into the kitchen to grab my plate.

By the time I sit down beside her, Bridget is munching away happily on her chicken, and she gazes over at me with a serious expression.

"I don't say this lightly, but I'm pretty sure this is the best meal I've ever eaten," she says, taking another bite of her food.

"Oh, what have I told you about being good for my ego?" I laugh. "What did you decide on watching?"

"I'm feeling like we go with one of the classics. What do you think about *Elf* or *Home Alone*?"

"They're both good, but *Elf* is my favorite," I admit.

"*Elf* it is then," she says, grabbing the remote and starting the movie.

We finish eating in comfortable silence, and once we're finished, we pause the movie briefly for me to take our plates to the kitchen and refill our wine.

"Here you go," I say, handing her back her glass of moscato.

"Thanks," she says sleepily, taking the glass from me before leaning down to pat her sleeping dogs on the head.

She sips her wine as she presses play on the movie, and I reach out my arm, gesturing for her to move closer to me. She obliges, sitting down her glass on the table beside her before she curls up against my side and rests her head in my lap. I absentmindedly run my fingers through her hair, and after a few minutes, I look down to see her sleeping peacefully.

I continue to toy with her hair, and as I look down at her, all the moments we've shared since I moved to town start to flash through my mind—months of nightly talks in the kitchen at the inn, the way she looked when she walked down the aisle toward me, and the nights we've spent cuddling close to each other under the covers.

As these moments play on repeat in my brain, it hits me that, without meaning to, I've fallen in love with Bridget.

A small part of my brain warns me that it's too soon to have such strong feelings for this girl, but as soon as the thought crosses my mind, I know it's not true.

Bridget has turned my quiet life upside down over the last week, and the thought of returning to my small bachelor pad apartment at the end of this feels incredibly depressing.

I take a breath, allowing myself to come to terms with this realization before sighing.

I know Bridget and I agreed to figure everything out after Christmas, but I can't pretend that there's any way I can let her walk away in just three days.

All that I can do is hope she feels the same way.

CHAPTER 13
BRIDGET

"I think we should put the hot chocolate booth closest to the entrance. What do you think?" I ask Millie as we put the finishing touches on the Candy Cane Carnival the following afternoon.

"I think that sounds good," she agrees, looking down at the vendor map we finalized several weeks ago.

"I can't believe how many people signed up to sell goodies this year," Millie adds, and I nod in agreement.

Aside from a number of games for the kids and a few local artisans hosting art classes for the adults, we added over forty vendors selling everything from jewelry to small art pieces to fun Christmas treats.

"It's gonna be a great event. How was the town Christmas movie last night?" I ask, straightening the sign on the entrance.

"It was really good. A lot of the families told me they enjoyed it, and the new pizza place in town really knocked it out of the park with the concessions," Millie says.

"Oh, I can't wait to try it. So, we haven't gotten a chance

to talk since you got back. How was New York?" I ask, turning back to face my best friend.

"We just had the best time, even despite all the weather mishaps. I don't think I'd necessarily like living there, but it was perfect for a long vacation."

"Good, I'm glad y'all had fun," I tell her honestly.

"Enough about me. I want to know more about you and Easton," Millie sings, winking at me.

"Ugh, I don't know, Mills," I sigh. "I think I'm really in trouble."

"Wait, why?" Millie asks, her eyes wide. "Did something happen?"

"Nothing bad," I promise. "I just really like him, but technically all this ends in just a few days. We only agreed to keep everything going through Christmas."

"Is that what you want?" Millie asks, and I shake my head.

"No, that's the problem."

"I see," Millie sighs, wrapping her arm around me. "The whole falling in love process is exhilarating, but no one really talks about how scary it is."

"Love?" I squeak, looking at her in surprise. "Who said anything about love? We only started this whole thing a week ago."

"So? That's about all it took for me to fall head over heels for your cousin. And he was a stranger. You and Easton have been friends for months."

I listen to her words, and I open my mouth to argue before I realize she's right. I've known for a few days that what I'm feeling for my fake husband is more than a crush, but I haven't wanted to admit it, even to myself.

"Yeah, I guess," I sigh, trying to come to terms with the fact that I'm in love with Easton Morgan

"I know," Millie says, taking in the look on my face. "But I promise, if you can push past the fear, it's the best feeling in the world."

"What if he doesn't feel the same way?" I ask, unable to help myself.

"You can't worry about that. All you can worry about is how you feel," Millie replies.

"What about the inn?" I ask, going through all the excuses I've come up with in my head for why we can't be together.

"Well, if you haven't noticed, Brian and I don't really have a policy on not dating your coworkers."

I laugh, unable to help myself. "Okay, well, that may be true, but I'm kind of his boss."

Millie shrugs. "Brian was completely my boss when everything started with us. It worked out just fine for us."

"Remind me not to put you in charge of any of the HR talks anytime soon," I tease, and Millie rolls her eyes.

"I get what you're saying. Really, I do. But while you and Brian co-manage the inn, Easton technically doesn't report to any of us. Yes, we hired him, but he runs everything in the restaurant without any real oversight from any of us."

"That's true," I concede.

"Looks like you have a lot to think about," Millie says, and I nod.

"But first, we have a bouncy house to set up," I say, and Millie laughs.

"I guess we'd better get to it then."

"THIS IS INCREDIBLE," EASTON SAYS, LOOKING AROUND AT THE Candy Cane Carnival later that night. "It's hard to believe that tomorrow is Christmas Eve," he adds.

I nod at his words, trying not to think too hard about what that means for us. The last week was a peek into the life we could have together, and now that I've had a taste, I don't want to go back to quiet nights in my small townhouse.

"I know. These last few days have really flown by," I agree. "I have to admit, I wouldn't mind if time could slow down just a little bit."

"Why's that?" he asks, pulling my hand to his lips and dropping a gentle kiss on my knuckles.

"Because, I don't think I'm ready for this to end," I whisper.

He looks at me as if he's trying to make sure he heard me correctly.

"Wait, really?" he asks, refusing to look away from me.

"Yes, really," I say with a nod. "But I've gotta say, I'm scared, Easton."

"Scared of what?" he asks, looking at me in confusion.

"I'm scared of losing you, but I'm also scared of change," I admit. "I've really come to value your friendship, and Brian would never forgive me if I did anything to push you away or caused you to leave the inn."

"I'm not going anywhere," Easton promises quickly. "Even if something happens between us, which I don't think it will, then I'll stay. I can't promise you everything will always be perfect between us, but I can promise there's nothing you could do that would push me away like that. I love working for Deer Valley, and I love living in Springside. But aside from that, the truth is, Bridget, I'm completely in love with you," he says, and I blink at him in shock.

"What?" I squeak out.

"I'm in love with you, Bridget," he says. "You don't have to say it back, but I can't let this end in a few days without you knowing how I feel about you."

"Easton," I say, holding up my hand. "That's not what I meant. I'm in love with you too. I just figured that since it happened so fast, there's no way you could feel the same way."

He smiles at me, taking in my words before dropping a hard kiss to my mouth.

"Hell yeah." He sighs, pulling me into his arms and spinning us around.

"Did you two finally pull your heads out of your asses and admit you're completely in love with each other?" Millie asks, smiling as she leads Brian over to where we're standing.

"Finally?" Easton says with a laugh. "We've only been fake married for a week."

"Easton, I hate to tell you, but we've been waiting for you and Bridget to realize that y'all were obsessed with each other for months," Millie says, rolling her eyes. "We figured y'all just needed a little push."

"Wait, what push?" I ask, narrowing my eyes.

"I may have asked Miss Ethel to spend the day of the wedding talking up the town Christmas events to Catherine. I figured if she decided to extend her stay, y'all would have to keep up the charade," Millie says with a shrug.

"This fucking town," I sigh. "But I guess it worked out okay this time," I say, pulling Easton down to kiss him.

"More than okay," he agrees, kissing me again just as Catherine makes her way over to us.

"Look at these two love birds," she says, smiling over at Easton and I.

"Hey there! How's your visit going?" I ask.

"Oh, everything's been wonderful," Catherine replies. "Now, I just have one question."

"Okay," I say hesitantly, looking over at Millie. She shrugs, letting me know she isn't in on this one.

"Whenever y'all decide to have your real wedding, would you make sure I'm included in the guest list?" Catherine asks, smirking at us.

Millie, Brian, Easton, and I stare at her in shock, until finally my brain kicks in, and I shake my head. "Wait. What do you mean? You were there for our real wedding," I argue, brushing a piece of my hair back nervously.

"Oh, Bridget. I spend all my time going to weddings for couples across the country. I know the difference between a couple who's been in love and a couple who's falling in love."

"Catherine, I—" Millie starts, but Catherine holds up her hand to stop her.

"I'm not upset. I attended a wonderful wedding of two people who I believe really are in love in one of the most charming little towns I've ever visited. And as far as the cover story goes, that's what I plan to say."

Millie nods at her gratefully, and Catherine turns her attention back to us. "I don't mean to be too forward, but whatever you two have is special. I've enjoyed getting to know you over the last few days, and I wish you two nothing but happiness."

"Thank you," I tell her truthfully. "We're really glad you stayed."

'Me too," Catherine says with a laugh. "Let me tell you, I do a lot of traveling for work, but I've never had a better gingerbread latte in my life. And that bakery downtown made the most delightful cookies I've ever tasted."

"This town is pretty special. You'd better watch out or you'll end up deciding to stay forever like I did," Millie says, smiling up at Brian who leans down to drop a kiss on her lips.

"We'll see about that," Catherine says with a laugh. "I don't think I found exactly what you did here in Springside, but maybe one day."

Her face turns a little wistful as she looks over at us before she shrugs it off. "Anyway, I'm off to do some shopping. I'll see you all tomorrow night at the Gingerbread Gala."

We wave at her as she leaves, and Easton pulls me into his arms again, kissing me hard.

"Who knew all this could come from getting married under the mistletoe?" I ask with a laugh.

Easton smiles, kissing me again before dropping another kiss to my forehead.

"Best decision I ever made," he says with a wink. "Now come on, I think there's some hot chocolate calling our name, Mrs. Morgan."

EPILOGUE
BRIDGET

SIX MONTHS LATER

"Good morning, Sugar," Easton says, dropping a kiss to my lips and handing me a cup of coffee. "Did you sleep well?"

"I did. I hate to admit it, but I think you were right about needing a vacation." I sigh, looking out the window at the perfect blue water outside our beachside bungalow.

"I'm always right, Mrs. Morgan," Easton teases, leaning down to pepper my face with kisses.

"I don't know about that." I laugh, shaking my head at him. "Also, you really should quit calling me that. It's been six months since our fake wedding, and there isn't anyone around to pretend for anymore."

"I could," Easton says with a shrug. "Or I could do this."

I gasp as he sinks beside the bed on one knee and pulls out a diamond wedding band that matches the one he gave me on our wedding day.

"Bridget, I'm absolutely in love with you. I never imagined I could be as completely obsessed with someone as I am with you. You make my days brighter, and there's nothing I wouldn't do for you. So, would you do me the honor of becoming Mrs. Morgan—for real this time?"

I sit up from the bed, staring at him in shock before nodding. "Of course I'll marry you," I agree, letting him slip the second band on my finger. It sits perfectly next to my other rings which I haven't bothered to take off, and I smile down at them before reaching out to pull Easton's mouth to mine.

His kiss is hot and desperate, and I pull him into bed with me, wrapping my legs around his waist as our tongues tangle.

"Can't wait to spend the rest of my life just like this," he mumbles, kissing down my neck.

"I like the sound of that," I agree, tugging his worn T-shirt over his head and running my fingers across his chest.

"God, I love you," he groans, pulling my oversized shirt off and leaning back to admire my naked body. "So fucking beautiful."

I feel the familiar blush creep into my cheeks at his praise before I pull him closer, tugging his pajama bottoms down.

"Does my sweet girl want my cock?" he asks, leaning in to drop kisses down my stomach before hovering over my pussy with his mouth.

"Yes," I beg, wrapping my legs around him in the effort to pull him closer.

"Sugar, I promise I'm gonna fuck you until you're dripping with my cum, but first I need a taste of your sweet pussy," he says, dropping kisses on my stomach and thighs.

"Please," I encourage him, desperate to feel him everywhere.

He looks up at me, keeping his eyes locked on mine as he starts to lick and suck at my clit.

"So fucking sweet," he whispers, nipping at my clit with his teeth and making me cry out in surprise before reaching up to grab my hips and flipping me so that my ass is in the air.

"I love seeing you like this," he murmurs, running his hands up and down my ass and the back of my thighs. "You're so pretty when you're desperate for my cock."

I whimper at his words, and he places his cock at my entrance, teasing me just enough to drive me wild.

"Do you want me to fuck you, Sugar?" he asks, continuing to run his hands up and down my ass.

"Yes. Easton, please," I cry, swirling my hips in the attempt to feel more of him.

He grabs both of my hips, holding me still as he slides slowly inside me. We both groan as soon as he's fully inside me and he leans down to kiss my bare back.

"Never gonna get enough of this." He sighs, starting to move his hips faster. He's so deep this way, and I feel myself start tighten around him as he fucks me hard.

His thrusts become more and more frantic, and he leans down, reaching around me to lightly pinch my nipple. I cry out at the sensation as he continues to fuck me.

"Come for me, Mrs. Morgan. I want to feel my wife come apart on my cock."

His words are the final push I need, and my orgasm hits me hard. I lose myself to the feeling, and it's only a few more seconds before I feel his release start to coat my walls.

His movements slow as we both struggle to catch our breath until he finally pulls out of me.

"This sight never gets old," he whispers, leaning down to

catch his cum as it drips out of me before using his finger to push it back inside me.

"Easton," I cry, overly sensitive from the orgasm I just had.

I look back at him, and he winks at me before leaning down and lifting me from the bed to carry me to the shower.

He turns the water on and lets it heat up before placing me on my feet and climbing into the warm shower with me.

"I can't tell you how happy you make me," he says, pulling me into his arms and dropping a gentle kiss on my lips before he starts to wash my hair.

"Back at you," I say truthfully. "Sometimes I still can't believe this is real."

"I know what you mean," Easton agrees, massaging the shampoo into my scalp. "But now that I have you, I know I'm not ever letting you go."

"I'm okay with that," I say with a smile. "So, what do you want to do today?"

"Well, I figured we could grab breakfast from the place down the street that you liked, and then we could spend the day by the water."

"That sounds good to me," I agree. "I promise to relax today, but after that, we've got a wedding to plan."

"Here we go again." Easton laughs, turning me around to drop a gentle kiss on my lips. "But you'd better make sure this one is perfect because I intend for this one to last forever."

ACKNOWLEDGMENTS

Wow! I can't believe we're here already! There are so many people that make these books happen, and I couldn't be more grateful for I have such an incredible and supportive team.

First of all, C, you're the reason I write happily ever afters. Through all the ups and downs the last two years have thrown at us, I couldn't be more grateful for the steadfast way you love and support me. You are always the first person to encourage me to write these stories, and you're also the first to remind me that I'm human and need to put the computer down from time to time. Thank you for keeping me balanced and loving me so well.

Mom and Dad, I finally finished this one. Your support means the world to me, and none of this would be possible without your help. I'm so grateful for every packing party, signing roadtrip, and post office run.

Nonnie and Dah, thank you for shouting about my books to everyone you know and always reminding me how proud you are of me. I'm forever blessed to have you in my corner.

Cassie, all I can say is bless your heart. There is so much of this job that goes on behind the scenes, and I can't thank you enough for always picking up my slack. None of this would work without your help, and I couldn't ask for a better assistant.

To my author friends, specifically Ambar and Alexandra,

thank you so much for all the word count check ins and the moral support during this one. I adore you both endlessly.

Caroline, you are the sweetest angel proofreader I could ask for and I am forever grateful that you put up with my chaos.

Rae, thank you so much for helping manage my releases! I am so grateful for all your help with ARCs, and I am so grateful for your organization and encouragement.

For the beta readers who put up with the absolute chaos I dropped in the doc, thank you.

To my sweet ARC readers, thank you so much for believing in my stories. Every share, repost, and comment means the world to me, and I can't say thank you enough for helping me share this story.

And finally, to you sweet reader, thank you for picking up this book. Absolutely none of this would be possible without you, and I adore you endlessly for taking a chance on Bridget and Easton's story.

FULL LIST OF CONTENT WARNINGS

Explicit Language
Explicit Sexual Content

BE THE FIRST TO KNOW

Want to stay up to date on all the things? Join my
newsletter, sign up for alerts on upcoming signings, and
follow my reader group here!

ABOUT THE AUTHOR

Hollie Luckie is a small town girl that wholeheartedly believes in happily ever afters. Between reading and writing romance, she is always getting lost in a fictional world. She resides in south Alabama with her high school sweetheart, her dog Memphis, and her own farm of quirky farm animals. You can find Hollie on Instagram at @authorhollieluckie or on Goodreads.

ALSO BY HOLLIE LUCKIE

Springside Series

Where We Break

Why We Break

What We Build

Deer Valley Inn Holiday Novellas

Matchmaking Under The Mistletoe

Married Under The Mistletoe

Crestbrook Cove

Searching for Sunshine

WTS (Coming Summer 2026)

Mills Corner

Secrets and Spurs

www.ingramcontent.com/pod-product-compliance
Lightning Source LLC
Chambersburg PA
CBHW050424110726
47899CB00008B/2840